INVISIBLE FIENDS

RAGGY MAGGIE

BARRY HUTCHISON

INVISIBLE FIENDS

RAGGY MAGGIE

HarperCollins *Children's Books*

First published in paperback in Great Britain by
HarperCollins *Children's Books* 2010

HarperCollins *Children's Books* is a division of HarperCollins*Publishers* Ltd
77-85 Fulham Palace Road, Hammersmith, London W6 8JB

Visit us on the web at www.harpercollins.co.uk
Visit Barry at www.barryhutchison.com

Text copyright © Barry Hutchison 2010

ISBN 978-0-00-731516-1

Barry Hutchison reserves the right to be identified as the author of the work.

Printed and bound in England by Clays Ltd, St Ives plc

Mixed Sources
Product group from well-managed
forests and other controlled sources
www.fsc.org Cert no. SW-COC-001806
© 1996 Forest Stewardship Council

FSC is a non-profit international organisation established to promote the
responsible management of the world's forests. Products carrying the FSC
label are independently certified to assure consumers that they come
from forests that are managed to meet the social, economic and
ecological needs of present and future generations.

Find out more about HarperCollins and the environment at
www.harpercollins.co.uk/green

To Mum and Dad.

For believing, even when I didn't, and for

having confidence when I had none.

Oh, and for all the food and money.

PROLOGUE

What had I expected to see? I wasn't sure. An empty street. One or two late-night wanderers, maybe.

But not this. Never this.

There were hundreds of them. *Thousands.* They scuttled and scurried through the darkness, swarming over the village like an infection, relentless and unstoppable.

I leaned closer to the window and looked down at the front of the hospital. One of the larger creatures was tearing through the fence, its claws slicing through the wrought-iron bars as if they were cardboard. My breath fogged the glass and the monster vanished behind a cloud of condensation. By the time the pane cleared the *thing* would be inside the hospital. It would be up the stairs in moments. Everyone in here was as good as dead.

The distant thunder of gunfire ricocheted from somewhere near the village centre. A scream followed – short and sharp, then suddenly silenced. There were no more gunshots after that, just the triumphant roar of something sickening and grotesque.

I heard Ameena take a step closer behind me. I didn't need to look at her reflection in the window to know how terrified she was. The crack in her voice said it all.

'It's the same everywhere,' she whispered.

I nodded slowly. 'The town as well?'

She hesitated long enough for me to realise what she meant. I turned away from the devastation outside. 'Wait… You really mean *everywhere*, don't you?'

Her only reply was a single nod of her head.

'*Liar!*' I snapped. It couldn't be true. This couldn't be happening.

She stooped and picked up the TV remote from the day-room coffee table. It shook in her hand as she held it out to me.

'See for yourself.'

Hesitantly, I took the remote. 'What channel?'

She glanced at the ceiling, steadying her voice. 'Any of them.'

The old television set gave a faint *clunk* as I switched it on. In a few seconds, an all-too-familiar scene appeared.

Hundreds of the creatures. Cars and buildings ablaze. People screaming. People running. People *dying*.

Hell on Earth.

'That's New York,' she said.

Click. Another channel, but the footage was almost identical.

'London.'

Click.

'I'm… I'm not sure. Somewhere in Japan. Tokyo, maybe?'

It could have been Tokyo, but then again it could have been anywhere. I clicked through half a dozen more channels, but the images were always the same.

'It happened,' I gasped. 'It actually happened.'

I turned back to the window and gazed out. The clouds above the next town were tinged with orange and red. It was already burning. They were destroying everything, just like *he'd* told me they would.

This was it.

The world was ending.

Armageddon.

And it was all my fault.

TWENTY-THREE DAYS
EARLIER...

Chapter One

I DON'T LIKE MONDAYS

I awoke with a start, clutching at my covers, my skin slippery with sweat. It was the dream again. The long, dimly lit corridor. The locked door. The *clop-ssshk* of strange, unknown footsteps chasing me, then the soft giggle as I was dragged down into the darkness. The same story, night after night after night.

As always, the details of the dream quickly began to fade. I usually remembered the bigger things – the lights in the corridor going off; the grey, shapeless figure battering against the windows; even the voices on the other side of the locked door. It was the little details that got lost. I always remembered the voices whispering to me, but I could never recall a single word of what they actually said. Hopefully it wasn't anything important.

I lay there for several minutes, slowly letting myself come round. There'd be no getting back to sleep, but lazing in bed for a few hours would be better than nothing.

Assuming I had a few hours. I had no idea what time it was. It was dark outside, but that didn't help at all. It was early January, and dark until almost half past eight these days.

From the corner of my eye I could make out the red glow of my radio alarm clock. I couldn't bring myself to turn and look at it. If I did then I might discover I had to get out of bed, and that was something I wasn't ready to do. Not yet.

There were noises downstairs. That had to be bad news. The rattling of plates meant Mum was up, and the burning smell meant she was making breakfast. It would soon be time.

I shuddered at the thought of what awaited me today,

and snuggled down into my covers. Despite the dream, right at that moment I felt completely safe and secure – something I hadn't felt in a fortnight now. I pulled the duvet up to my chin, wanting to prolong the sense of security for as long as I could.

It had been less than two weeks since Christmas Day. Less than two weeks since "The Incident". Since then, I'd been constantly on edge, always expecting something to come jumping out of the shadows, or crashing through my bedroom window.

But there had been nothing. No monsters. No journeys to other worlds. No cryptic messages from long-lost relatives. Nothing.

As the days passed, the sense of dread faded a little, only to be replaced by a new creeping terror. Another nightmare had been drawing steadily closer, and now it loomed on the horizon. Something that promised to be almost as bad as Christmas Day had been. Something *horrible*.

'Kyle,' Mum shouted from the bottom of the stairs. 'It's time to get up.'

I groaned into my pillow, knowing there was no way of escaping my fate. Knowing without doubt that the time had finally come.

Raising my head, I looked in the direction of my bedroom door. Through the gloom I could make out a grey shape hanging there, its long, thin arms flapping loosely down by its sides.

My shirt. Mum had ironed it. That confirmed things. The holidays were officially over.

It was time to go back to school.

Mum was scraping the black bits off a slice of toast when I shuffled into the kitchen, tucking my shirt into the itchy grey trousers of my uniform. She had quite a fight on her hands – the toast seemed to be nothing *but* black bits.

'I made you toast,' she said, 'but it might be a bit... crispy.'

I caught sight of another few slices of burned bread and headed for the food cupboard. 'I'll just have cornflakes.'

'Suit yourself,' Mum shrugged, but I could tell she was secretly relieved. She let the toast drop into the bin, then turned to face me. I could feel her watching my every move as I poured myself the final dregs from the cornflakes box and sloshed them with the last of the milk.

She waited until I had crammed the first spoonful into my mouth before she started to speak.

'Excited about going back?'

I couldn't reply, so I just shrugged.

'It'll be fun,' she smiled. 'It'll do you good to get out of the house and mixing again. You've hardly set foot outside the door since...' The sentence was left hanging there. 'It'll be fun,' she repeated, at last.

Mum didn't like talking about what had happened. I'd tried to bring it up in the days after Christmas, but she'd always changed the subject. Now I didn't even bother to mention it, because I couldn't stand the awkward silences it created.

'We've got a visitor this afternoon,' she said, forcing a smile. 'Little Lilly from down the road. I'm babysitting.'

'Little Lilly who?' I asked, through a mouthful of cereal.

'Lilly Gibb. She's three. Angela's little one.'

That didn't help. I didn't even know who Angela was. 'What does she look like?' I asked.

'You've seen her before. Little girl. Blonde hair,' Mum said. 'Isn't her brother in your class? Billy, I think.'

'Billy Gibb's sister's called Lilly?' I snorted. 'Billy and Lilly. Very imaginative.'

Mum's smile was thin-lipped. 'Not everyone has your imagination.'

She wasn't wrong there. I doubted anyone had an imagination quite like mine. Lucky for them.

'She won't be here for long, will she?' I asked. I couldn't be bothered with a little kid running around the house.

'Just an hour or so after you get home,' she said. I must've pulled a face or something, because she followed up with: 'I know, honey, but... well, the money'll come in handy.'

I nodded and adjusted my face into something resembling a smile. 'It's fine,' I said, then I stuffed some more cornflakes into my mouth to stop me saying anything else.

I chewed in silence for a few moments. Mum was watching me. I could tell by the way she was breathing she was building up to saying something.

'You know you can't tell anyone?' she finally said.

I swallowed down the soggy milky mush. 'About babysitting Lilly Gibb?'

'No, about what happened. About any of it.'

'I was kidding,' I said. 'I know.'

'Right. Because they wouldn't understand,' she continued. 'It'd cause... problems.'

'You mean they'd think I was mental.'

She smiled. 'I'm sure they wouldn't think…' Her voice cracked and her head suddenly dropped. When she looked up again she was ten years older. 'It's over now, sweetheart,' she whispered. 'You can put it behind you. We all can.'

I nodded in what I hoped would be a reassuring way. Inside, though, I knew she was wrong. 'It begins.' That's what had been written on the card my dad had left for me.

Whatever was happening, it was far from over. Christmas had just been the start. I didn't know what danger awaited me. I didn't know what horrors I was going to face. I just knew something was going to happen, and I had a horrible suspicion it was going to happen soon.

'Have fun!' chirped Mum from the kitchen, as I pulled my red school jumper over my head, slung my bag over my shoulder and headed out into the hall. I got there in time to see a bundle of junk mail spew through the letterbox and spatter on to the mat.

'Will do. Post's here,' I replied, kneeling to pick it up. 'I'll put it on the side.' I flicked through the envelopes, looking for anything with my name on the front. There was nothing. I didn't know whether to be relieved or disappointed.

As I moved to stand up, my gaze drew level with the letterbox. Two chubby fingers held it propped open. A pair of eyes stared in at me through the gap.

'Um... hey, Hector,' I said, recognising our postman from his grey eyebrows and wrinkled, weather-beaten skin. He watched me, unblinking. 'You OK?' I continued. 'What... what are you doing?'

His gaze continued to bore into me, making me uncomfortable. Hector could be a bit quirky sometimes – that was part of what made him so popular on the street – but even for him, this was extra weird.

When he finally spoke, his voice was low and lifeless,

lacking its usual colour: 'Peek-a-boo,' he muttered. 'I see you.'

Slowly, without another word, he let the letterbox creak back down into place. A second later, I heard him break into his familiar whistle as he walked back along the garden path.

Unsure of what had just happened, I stayed where I was – kneeling on the floor – until the whistling had faded into the distance. Hector's weirdness shouldn't have bothered me, but for some reason my heart was pumping like it was about to break out of my chest.

'What are you doing?' demanded Mum. Her voice made me jump upright in fright. I turned and saw her standing in the kitchen doorway, her hands on the hips of her pale brown dressing gown. 'You'll miss the bus. You're going to be late for school.'

Mum was right. I *was* late for my first lesson, English,

though not by much. The fact I arrived only two minutes after class had started didn't seem to matter to Mr Preston, though. He was lounging in his chair with his hands behind his head when I stumbled my way into his classroom.

'Well, well, speak of the devil,' tutted the teacher, swivelling his seat to face me. 'We were just discussing you, Mr Alexander.'

I glanced at the neatly spaced rows of not-so-friendly faces sitting in front of me and felt my cheeks redden with embarrassment.

'Sorry I'm late,' I offered, making a move towards the one empty desk in the class.

'Not so fast there,' Mr Preston said. His chair gave a squeak as he leaned forwards and stood up. His fingers brushed the polished surface of the motorbike helmet that sat, in pride of place, on his desk, then he shuffled lazily across to the blackboard.

Mr Preston is into motorbikes in a big way. I know this

because he spends at least one whole lesson a week talking in excruciating detail about his own motorcycle. Once he joked that he loves the bike more than he loves his wife.

At least, I think he was joking.

The rest of the class and I watched as he chalked the words *'What I Did in the Holidays'* on to the board.

'To break us in gently, we were about to discuss what we did during the Christmas break,' he explained, turning to face me. 'Since you're already up on your feet, perhaps you'd do us the honour of going first?

Chapter Two

BILLY GIBB

My cheeks felt like they were burning. I don't like talking in front of people. I reckon if I'm ever forced to choose between speaking in public and having my fingernails torn out with pliers, I'll have to give both options some really serious thought.

'I didn't do much,' I shrugged, hoping that would be enough to get me off the hook. Of course, it wasn't.

'You didn't do much?' Mr Preston smirked. He half sat, half leaned on his desk, both hands now in his pockets. 'Surely you can give us a bit more to go on than that?'

My mind raced. What could I say to get this over and

done with quickly? I had to be careful not to reveal anything about Christmas Day itself, but I had to tell him *something*.

'I... met a friend. A girl friend. I mean not a... Just a friend. Who's a girl.'

As one, the class erupted into a chorus of '*Ooohs*'.

'Who was it, your *gran*?' called a voice from the back of the class. I recognised it as Billy Gibb. I'd know those smug tones anywhere.

Billy had a lot of muscle, but not much going on between the ears. He'd been kept back for two years in primary school, and so was much older – and bigger – than anyone else in class. The first time he had been forced to repeat the year on account of having had too many days off. And then, two years after that, he'd been kept back again. On account of being thick.

'Quieten down,' Mr Preston warned, giving the entire class one of his glares. As silence fell, he turned back to me. 'I'm not sure if I want to hear the details or not,' he frowned, 'but carry on.'

I hesitated, boxing off in my head all the things I didn't dare reveal about Ameena, the girl who had saved my life. I realised quite quickly that what was left wasn't very interesting at all.

'Nothing to tell, really,' I said. 'Just met her at Christmas.'

'Where'd you meet her?' demanded one of the other boys sitting near Billy.

Another pause. Telling them she'd saved me from being strangled to death on my front doorstep wasn't really an option, even if it was the truth.

Christmas Day felt more and more like some distant, half-remembered nightmare. It had been no dream, though. It had happened. All of it.

I was alone in the house when he'd appeared, crashing through the living-room window in a shower of broken glass. Mr Mumbles had been my childhood imaginary friend. He'd been my funny little buddy, accompanying me everywhere I went. As I grew up I forgot all about him. Turned out he wasn't happy about that.

When he came back he was different. Bigger. Stronger. His body and face twisted and disfigured. This time round he wasn't interested in being friends. He had one goal and one goal only.

Killing me.

He would've managed too, had it not been for Ameena. She had appeared like an avenging angel, charging out of the darkness, swinging wildly with a baseball bat. She drove him back, buying us time to get away.

She'd stayed with me for most of the day, helping me when no one else could. How many times did she save my life? Twice? Three times? I couldn't even remember.

Without her I never would have beaten Mr Mumbles. I

owed her everything – my life, Mum's, Nan's. We all would have died had it not been for Ameena.

But I couldn't tell the class that.

'Earth to Kyle. Earth to Kyle.'

I blinked back into the present. Mr Preston was standing there, waving a hand slowly in front of my face. I could feel all eyes in the room on me. Somewhere off to the left, someone let out a low snigger.

'Just bumped into her outside my house,' I said. 'We... we hung out for a bit.'

'What was her name then?' asked someone else.

'Ameena,' I replied. My mouth was going dry. I felt like I was being interrogated by the Secret Service.

'What kind of name's that?'

'A made-up one by the sounds of things,' sneered Billy. He and his neighbour cackled and exchanged a high-five. I glanced up at Mr Preston imploringly, but he wasn't ready to let me off the hook just yet.

'And where is she now?' he asked, the corners of his mouth twitching. 'This new friend of yours?'

I was free to answer truthfully this time. 'I don't know. I didn't see her again after that.'

Mr Preston took his hands out of his pockets and waved them as if he was conducting an orchestra. 'Ready, everyone? One, two, three...'

On cue, the whole class joined together in one collective 'Awwww!'

'Fascinating stuff, Mr Alexander, truly fascinating,' said Mr Preston sarcastically. 'Now sit down, and please – for your sake as well as mine – don't be late again.'

I shuffled sideways along the slow-moving line, holding my breath when I passed the soggy mound of cabbage that seemed to be crawling up and out of the plastic tub it lurked in.

Turkey burgers – I could hardly believe it. The first day

back to school after the Christmas holidays and the canteen was serving turkey burgers. Someone somewhere had decided this was the perfect choice for the first-day-back menu. Incredible.

'You not meeting your new bird for lunch then?' I heard someone shout.

Billy Gibb had barged into the queue a few places ahead of me. He was staring at me now, waiting for some kind of response. I just shook my head and looked down at my cracked wooden tray. I didn't need this. Not today.

I could spend all day describing the things that made Billy such an unpleasant person to be around. I could talk about his stupid, wispy facial hair. I could mention the way his nostrils were always flared and curving upwards, as if a dog had taken a crap on his top lip and his nose was doing its best to crawl away. I could even go on about his smell – fifty per cent stale cigarette smoke, fifty per cent even staler sweat, one hundred per cent revolting.

Really, though, what bothered me most was his personality. Or, to put it more accurately, his total lack of one.

'She must've been a right dog to fancy you,' he continued, trying to goad me into a fight. I wasn't going to rise to it. I was better than that. Plus, he could kick my head in with one leg tied behind his back.

I heard him and a few of his mates jeering at me as I picked up my tray and walked away, but I tried not to listen. The healthy-eating counter didn't have a queue – the healthy-eating counter *never* had a queue – so I could hopefully get served there and have my lunch eaten before he'd even ordered his.

The dinner lady on duty had her back to me as I approached. I waited patiently at the counter. I didn't dare say anything, in case the shock of having a customer in this part of the canteen killed her stone dead.

After almost a minute, when she still showed no sign of turning in my direction, I gave a low, gentle cough.

That seemed to do the trick. With her two-sizes-too-small nylon uniform almost bursting at the seams, she at last shuffled round to look at me. Well, not exactly *look*. As she turned, I could see she was holding a chipped and dirty plate in front of her, completely hiding her face.

'Um... hi,' I began, assuming she'd move the plate when I started speaking. 'Have you got anything that's *quite* healthy, but not *too* healthy?' The plate didn't move. Maybe this was what being stuck on the healthy-eating counter all day did to you.

'Like, do you do low-fat hot dogs or something? Or veggie burgers, but with, like, a little bit of meat in them?'

She just stood there, not responding, the plate not moving. I glanced across at the rest of the canteen. Everyone was going about their own business – ordering lunches, scoffing food, stuffing chips up smaller kids' noses. No one was paying me or Plate Face the slightest bit of attention.

'Er... hello?' I tried. 'Can you hear me?'

A low breath escaped her lips, like the ominous rumblings of a once dormant volcano. Slowly, she leaned her head a little to the right, as she tilted the plate slightly to the left. A single eye peered at me from around the cracked crockery's edge.

'Peek-a-boo,' she whispered. 'I seeeee you.'

The plate slipped from her fingers. A roar of delight went up from the kids in the canteen as the crockery shattered loudly on the patterned linoleum floor.

'Nice work killing the dinner lady,' grinned Billy, punctuating the sentence by punching me hard on the arm.

'I didn't kill her,' I told him, pulling my schoolbag higher up on to my shoulder and quickening my pace along the science corridor. 'She fainted.'

She *had* fainted. The second the plate had shattered on the ground, she'd kind of slumped down, like a puppet whose strings had all snapped. Complete pandemonium had followed, with the teachers all trying to help her up, and the pupils all falling over each other to take photos on their mobiles.

Most of the kids had been laughing, or chattering excitedly. Not me. There was something unsettling about the way the dinner lady had behaved. And what she'd said to me – she'd spoken the same words as Hector the postman had spoken this morning. Something was happening, I knew, but what that something was I had no idea.

Two of Billy's friends rushed up to join him, and all thoughts of the dinner lady and the postie melted away. The three boys surrounded me – a minion on each side, Billy walking backwards in front of me.

'Must've been your way with women,' one of the lackeys snickered.

'Or his smell,' Billy suggested. All three of them laughed

at that. I wanted to tell Billy I couldn't possibly stink as badly as he did, but on the other hand I also wanted to live to see my next birthday.

Around us, other kids hurried on their way, not one of them so much as glancing in my direction as they scuttled past. I wasn't expecting anyone to jump in and save me, but even a bit of supportive eye contact from someone would have been nice.

Every few steps, Billy would jab one of his sausage-like fingers into my shoulder. Each time was harder than the one before. I had to get him talking and get his mind off pushing me around, before he did me some serious damage.

'My mum's babysitting your little sister today,' I said.

'I know. My mum's paying her twenty quid to do it.' Billy's face stretched into a mocking grin. 'She says she feels sorry for your mum because she's too useless to get a proper job. It's like charity, she says, since you're so poor.'

I felt my teeth clamp together and my fingers curl into fists. I didn't mind him pushing me around. I could take that. But not my mum. Nobody made fun of my mum.

I stopped dead. The other boys carried on a few paces before they realised what had happened. Billy stopped, then looked me up and down, pausing briefly at my clenched fists. 'Oh yeah?' he sneered.

All three of them stepped in close to me, looming above me. Billy was right in my face, his nose next to mine, his stinking breath swirling up my nostrils. I stared up into his narrowed eyes, not flinching.

The other two were right at my sides. There was no way I could swing a punch without them stopping it. They were both poised, ready to grab my arms. Ready to hold me while Billy pummelled.

I felt my nerve go. The anger that had burned through me was snuffed out by a wave of fear.

'You want to say something to me?' Billy snarled. 'Eh?'

I wanted to say a lot of things to him, but I didn't dare. He made a sharp move towards me and I flinched. All three boys laughed at that.

'So?' he hissed. 'What was it you wanted to say?'

My mind raced. My mouth went dry. I had to think of something to say, and fast.

And then I remembered – well, not exactly *remembered*, because the experience was one I would never, ever be able to forget. Right then, though, was the first time I'd put two and two together properly.

While hiding from Mr Mumbles I'd somehow transported myself to somewhere called the Darkest Corners. It was a horrible, terrifying place, full of horrible, terrifying creatures. That was where I'd met the girl.

She couldn't have been more than five years old, but something about her had chilled me to the bone. Her skin was as pale as death, but caked here and there with thick blobs of make-up. A smear of lipstick across her mouth.

Rings of black shadow around her eyes. A little girl playing at dressing up.

She had mentioned Billy. Or a Billy, at least. I doubted she was talking about this one, but it was worth a shot.

'I met another girl I think you might know,' I said shakily.

'Wouldn't surprise me,' Billy crowed. 'I know a lot of girls. What did she look like?'

He stepped back a little, so I quickly continued.

'She was young,' I said. 'Maybe five or something?' I glanced up at him. 'She had a doll.'

'A doll?' he snorted. 'Don't know who you're talking about.'

'Weird-looking thing. The doll, I mean. The girl too, actually. What was her name again...?' I wracked my brains. 'Caddie,' I announced. 'That was it.'

The colour drained from Billy's face, leaving him an ashen shade of grey. He eyeballed me, his head shaking ever so slightly from side to side.

'Who told you about that?' he demanded.

'No one,' I answered. 'I met her. She asked if I knew you, said that you used to play with her or something.'

'Shut up,' Billy hissed. 'You can't... You... Who've you been talking to?'

I smiled nervously. Billy looked like a bomb about to explode, and I was standing directly in his path. 'No one,' I insisted. 'I wasn't speaking to any—'

The punch crunched into the soft bit between my stomach and my chest, and I felt my lungs instantly cramp up. Before I realised what was happening, Billy had me by the front of my shirt. He was shouting something, but all my attention was focused on trying to draw a breath, and I missed most of what he said.

'...*ever* talk about that again,' was the only bit I caught, before he pushed me to the floor and stalked off, his two minions following close behind.

Fighting the urge to puke, I crouched on the floor, feeling my breath gradually return. A few of my classmates glanced pityingly at me as they rushed past, but none of them bothered to stop.

Then, just as I had begun to think about getting up, a hand reached down, palm upwards. I looked at it, then up into eyes I hadn't seen in a fortnight.

'OK,' frowned Ameena. 'And you let that jerk get away with that because...?'

Chapter Three

FAMILIAR FACES

I let Ameena help me up, then stood there brushing myself down, not quite sure what to say to her. I'd begun to think I would never see her again, and now I couldn't decide whether to hug her or shout at her. I decided, for the moment, to do neither.

She looked just as she had done when we'd first met, only now her long dark brown hair wasn't matted to her face with rain, and her deep brown eyes weren't wide with panic. She still wore the same shabby black jacket and jumper; still had the same oversized walking boots on her feet; still looked like she needed a good meal.

Seeing her brought everything rushing back. Every feeling from Christmas Day – the pain, the fear – came washing over me, all hitting me at once, making my legs go shaky and my head go light.

'You should've kicked that guy's ass,' she told me, glaring along the corridor in the direction Billy had gone. 'Why didn't you?'

'Uh, well, because I *can't*? You saw the size of him.'

She looked at me like I was crazy. 'You're kidding, right?'

'No, I'm not kidding,' I said. 'He'd kill me.'

'What?' she spluttered. 'But... Christmas. The stuff you did. The stuff you can *do*.'

I pulled my bag back up on to my shoulder and set off along the corridor. 'I don't want to talk about it,' I said.

'Maybe not, but it happened,' she replied. 'I saw it.' She quickened her pace and stopped in front of me. 'What, you think that guy's anywhere near as tough as Mr Mu—'

'*Please*,' I implored, 'can we not do this right now?' I stepped past her and carried on towards my next class. 'I'll talk about it later, but just... not right now.'

She hesitated for a few moments, not following me. 'No can do,' she said at last. 'I'm leaving town. Just dropped in to say goodbye.'

I stopped; turned to face her. I wanted to ask her where she was going. I wanted to ask her *why* she was going. There were a dozen questions I'd have liked the answer to. In the end, though, I just said: 'Oh.'

'Try not to get too cut up about it,' she said sarcastically.

'No, I... it's... I thought you'd already moved on. I haven't seen you since... you know.' We stood there, several metres apart, all alone in the corridor. Virtually strangers.

'Where were you?' I asked, more forcibly than I'd intended.

'I've been around,' she shrugged. 'Just thought you might need some space after everything that happened.'

'What I needed was someone to talk to,' I told her.

'You had people to talk to. You mum. Your gran.'

'Mum didn't want to listen,' I said. 'And Nan... Nan doesn't make a lot of sense half the time.' I glanced down at the floor, then back up at her. 'I needed someone who'd been through it. But you weren't there.'

'Hey, kiddo, I'm not a counselling service,' Ameena shrugged. She folded her arms across her chest and shifted her weight on to one foot. She was about the same age as me, but insisted on calling me "kiddo". It drove me nuts.

'No. But I thought you were a friend.'

'Friends don't get you anywhere,' she scowled, before wincing slightly at the harshness of her words. 'Listen, you want to talk? Here I am.'

'I told you, not now,' I answered. 'Can we meet up later?'

'And I told *you*, I'm leaving.'

'Just ten minutes after school,' I said. 'Please.'

She looked at me for a few moments, then gave a sigh. 'Ten minutes, then I'm gone. I'll meet you outside.'

'OK,' I replied, fighting back a grin of delight. 'I better run.'

'Later.'

I gave her a goodbye nod, then hurried off towards my next class. Halfway along the corridor, I paused. 'Oh, and Ameena,' I said, turning round, 'it's good to see—'

But the corridor was empty. Ameena was already gone.

I started the first afternoon lesson – History – the same way I'd started the first class of the morning – late. The teacher, Mrs Ennis, didn't look impressed when I scurried in, but at least she didn't put me through any ritual humiliation before letting me take a seat.

It was a relief to see that Billy's desk at the back of the

class was empty. He skipped lessons quite a lot, and I was glad he'd chosen to give this one a miss. I'd had more than enough of him for one day.

The rest of the class were already studying a textbook by the time I got settled at my desk. I peeked across at the girl sitting next to me to find out what book we were supposed to be looking at, then began rummaging in my bag for my copy.

A faint, nervous knocking on the classroom door made everyone look up from their work. I ignored it, still busy looking for the book.

'Enter,' called Mrs Ennis, in the posh voice she only ever uses when inviting someone in, and I heard the door swing open just as I found the right textbook. As I pulled it out of my bag, I caught a glimpse of a first-year boy hurrying across the classroom, his face red with embarrassment. He thrust a note into Mrs Ennis's hands, and then quickly beat a retreat.

I flicked through the pages of my book, trying to find the right chapter. Most of my classmates had turned back to their work, leaving only the really nosey ones to watch Mrs Ennis unfold and read the note.

'Kyle Alexander,' she said. I looked up to find her looking back. 'The headmistress would like a word.'

Making my way along the deserted corridor, a sense of dread began to rise from the pit of my stomach. Whatever Mrs Milton wanted to see me for, it was unlikely to be good.

Classroom doors lined the walls on either side of me. Teachers' and pupils' voices drifted out of every one as I passed. I recognised some of them, but not all.

A clattering, jeering and the occasional sharp blast of a whistle could be heard from the gym hall, which was also accessed from this part of the school. The trophy cabinet stood proudly by the hall entrance, stocked with cups and shields and medals. My name wasn't etched on to any of them.

I pushed through the final set of double doors. A bleached, clinical smell wafted up to meet me as I headed towards the headmistress's office. This was usually as far as any parents made it into the school, so Mrs Milton made sure the janitor kept it sparkling clean.

I'd only been called to see the headmistress once before, and I'd been a gibbering mess of nerves by the time I'd made it down the first flight of stairs. No one ever got summoned for anything good. If Mrs Milton called for you, you could be pretty sure you were in serious trouble.

This time, though, I wasn't all that bothered. It'd be about the dinner lady, I was certain. She'd want to ask me what had happened, that was all. No harm in that. Nothing for me to worry about.

Morag the school secretary was sitting behind the reception desk as I approached, her eyes fixed on her computer screen. It was common knowledge that Morag could be used as a kind of barometer as to how bad

Mrs Milton's mood was. If she was smiling, things were unlikely to be *too* terrible. If she didn't make eye contact, you'd best get your will written before setting foot in the office.

'I'm supposed to see Mrs Milton,' I said, stopping in front of the reception desk. Morag looked up at me and beamed broadly. I was filled with relief.

'Ah yes, Kyle, isn't it?' she said. 'Just go through and wait in the office, she'll be in in a minute.'

'Thanks,' I said, returning the smile. I made for the office, a spring in my step. If I spun the story out, I could probably waste the entire lesson filling Mrs Milton in on what had happened. Maybe – if I really went into detail and repeated myself a bit – I could fill the whole afternoon. Not only would I avoid lessons, I'd also be able to avoid—

'Billy?' I frowned, as I eased open the door to the headmistress's office and stepped inside.

He was standing by the window, looking out through the

slatted wooden blinds. He whipped round at the sound of my voice, his eyes narrowing to slits when he saw me. 'What you doing here?' he demanded.

'I... a kid came in with a note,' I explained, feeling my confidence start to crumble. If Billy had been summoned too, then I wasn't here to talk about the dinner lady. It had to be about what had happened on the way to class. That wasn't good.

Mrs Milton was ruthlessly strict when it came to fighting in school, and I doubted she'd care that my only contribution to the "fight" was taking a punch to the guts.

Billy made a noise a bit like a horse sneezing and turned back to the window. 'We'll say we were just mucking about,' he instructed. He had obviously come to the same conclusion as I just had. 'It was nothing, just two mates having a laugh, all right?'

I stepped further into the room, but didn't answer. He turned and fixed me with a glare. 'All *right*?'

'Right,' I nodded. Like it or not, going along with him was the only way of cutting our losses. We'd probably still get into serious trouble, but not *fighting* serious.

We stood there for a while, neither of us speaking. Mrs Milton was taking her time. I suspected she might be waiting just outside the door, enjoying making us sweat. Teachers could be nasty like that, and head teachers in particular.

The office had been redecorated since the last time I was in it. The walls were covered in a cream wallpaper with a swirling design made up of varying shades of brown. A row of filing cabinets stood shoulder to shoulder along one of the walls, facing the high bookshelves that leaned against the wall directly opposite.

There was a thick carpet below me, also brown. As I looked down at it, I realised it was the only time I'd seen carpet in any part of the school. Maybe she got special treatment because she was the head. Or maybe all the teachers' areas were carpeted.

It struck me that there were whole areas of the school I'd never even seen inside. For all I knew, the staffroom could have disco balls hanging from the ceiling and tiger-skin rugs on the floor.

'So...' Billy said. He was still looking outside, but I knew what was coming next. 'Who told you?'

'About what?' I asked innocently.

'You know what.'

I should never have mentioned the girl and her doll. It had been a knee-jerk reaction to the threat of being beaten up. My meeting with Caddie definitely fell under the heading of "Things Not To Talk About".

'Your mum told my mum,' I lied. 'She told me.'

'I knew it,' he muttered, still not looking at me. I had a suspicion as to who the girl was, but wasn't sure whether to say anything and risk another beating. I decided to chance my luck.

'I had an invisible friend too,' I said. 'When I was young. It's nothing to be embarrassed about.'

He didn't answer, which itself told me all I needed to know.

'I'm not waiting round here any more,' he scowled, turning from the window. He barged past me on his way to the door.

'Are you sure that's a good idea?' I asked. I didn't like the idea of being the only one around for Mrs Milton to shout at.

'Tell her I was sick and had to go home,' he told me. 'Tell her anything, I don't care.'

I was about to reply when he yanked open the door. He drew up short as we both realised Mrs Milton really had been lurking just outside the office. She stood framed in the doorway, leaning slightly forward, her arms hanging limp and loose by her sides.

'Mrs M,' Billy smiled. 'There you are. I was just going to

come and look for...'

His voice trailed off. He'd realised what I had –
something was very wrong with Mrs Milton.

Her breathing was noisy; wheezy and rattling at the
back of her throat as she inhaled. Her face was as pale as
chalk dust, its expression blank and empty, like something
dead. Or something that had never been alive in the first
place.

Ringing her eyes were two circles of make-up; caked-on,
thick black swirls of tar. A streak of crimson lipstick was
smeared across her mouth, starting on one cheek and
finishing high up on the other. It stood out against her pale
skin like a raw, gaping wound. She looked frightening.
Grotesque.

And disturbingly familiar.

'I'm dressing up like Mummy,' spoke a voice from within
her. It was high-pitched and childish, and didn't belong to
her. 'Would you like to play?'

Chapter Four

TAG, YOU'RE IT

Even Billy, who was usually first with the wisecracks, said nothing. He took two paces backwards into the office, but otherwise showed no reaction to Mrs Milton's weirdness.

If the way she'd slapped on her make-up was familiar to me, though, Billy must've recognised it too. He *had* to. I'd only ever seen one other person with their face made up like that: Caddie.

Billy's invisible friend.

'Is this a wind-up?' I heard him mutter at last. There was a note to his voice I'd never heard before – uncertainty or panic, or something in between.

'I like playing,' trilled Mrs Milton. She was slowly twirling a curl of her mousy-brown hair round a finger; still speaking in a voice fifty years too young for her.

With a sudden lunge, she hopped into the room. Her eyes stayed fixed on Billy as she stood there, wobbling unsteadily on one leg. 'Do you like playing too?'

'Billy,' I said, in what came out as a hoarse whisper. 'Don't let her get too close.'

Billy snapped round at the sound of my voice, as if he'd forgotten I was even there in the room. 'What?' he demanded. 'Did you put her up to this?'

I shook my head. 'Nothing to do with me.'

Mrs Milton's blank gaze rounded on me. I could make out my own reflection in her eyes, but there was no other sign of life in them anywhere.

'Let's play a game,' she sang. With another hop she was in the middle of the office, right by her desk. I hurried backwards out of her reach, in case she decided to make a grab for me. My back bumped against the bookshelves and I shuffled along to where they ended. From there I had a clear path to the now unguarded doorway; an escape route, in case I needed to get out of there fast.

'What kind of game?' I asked her, stalling for time. Something was happening here, but I didn't quite understand what.

'What are you doing?' Billy spat. His eyes were shifting quickly from me to Mrs Milton and back again. 'Why are you even talking to her? She's clearly gone mental.'

The head teacher's lifeless eyes swivelled on him, her face still empty of all emotion. Billy stared right back. He was smirking, trying to act confident and unafraid, but the way his feet shuffled on the carpet told another story.

'Did you hear that, Mrs Milton?' he said. 'It's the pressure. You've gone nuts. They'll probably stick you in a home for the retarded.'

The words were classic Billy, but the delivery was off, as if he was a bad actor playing the role. He was terrified, but some subconscious autopilot inside him was determined not to show it.

'Just think,' he continued, 'you'll never be able to give me detention again.'

Her expression – or lack of it – remained fixed in place, but the finger in her hair began to twirl faster. My attention was so focused on that hand I didn't notice the other one creeping towards the penholder on the desk until it was too late.

'Mrs Milton isn't allowed out right now,' sing-songed the child's voice from deep within the adult's body. She brought her hand up from the desk. It was clutching a large pair of metal scissors. The light from the window glinted off the blades as she pointed them at Billy's throat. 'But I know a fun game we can play.'

'Billy, run.'

He hesitated, the smirk still fixed on his lips. 'What?'

I made a dive for the open door, catching his arm and dragging him along with me. 'I said *run*!'

We stumbled from the office together and out into the corridor. Just before we did, I caught a glimpse of Mrs Milton snipping at the air with the scissors. *Shnick-shnick-shnick.*

The reception area was empty when we scrambled past. No sign of Morag. No sign of anyone who could help.

'We've got to get out of here,' I said, and I began to drag Billy along the corridor towards the main door.

After just a few steps, he yanked his arm free and stopped in his tracks.

'What you doing?' he demanded.

I skidded to a stop a few paces on. 'We've got to get away from her,' I spluttered. 'We have to get help.'

Billy's face was a few shades paler than usual, but his arrogant sneer was back. 'You know, you nearly had me?'

he said. 'Just for a minute there, you nearly had me.'

'What are you talking about?' I glanced over his shoulder. There was no sign yet of Mrs Milton, but it would only be a matter of time.

'How did you get her to go along with it? That's what I want to know.'

'Go along with what?' I frowned. 'You don't still think this is a joke?'

Billy took a step closer. I could see his fingers were bunched into fists. 'Let me think,' he muttered. 'You talk about some little girl who you say was my imaginary friend – even though I never had an imaginary friend, since only losers have imaginary friends – and then suddenly you've got Milton acting like a five-year-old who wants to do me in with a pair of scissors.'

He rubbed his chin, pretending to be deep in thought. 'So yes, I do think it's a joke.' He took another step closer and raised a fist. 'And look – here comes the punch line.'

'Wait,' I cried. The sound echoed along the otherwise silent corridor. 'Listen.'

Billy paused, his fist held motionless up by his right ear. 'What? I don't hear anything.'

'Exactly.' I nodded in the direction of a set of doors a dozen or so metres further along the corridor. 'There should be a class in the gym hall.'

'So?'

'So why can't we hear them?'

He scowled and pulled his fist back sharply. 'Who cares?'

'Raggy Maggie!' I yelped, screwing shut my eyes and throwing up my hands for protection from a blow that never came.

'What... what did you say?'

I opened my eyes, but kept my guard up. Billy had taken a step back. His mouth was open, the rage on his face gone.

'Raggy Maggie,' I repeated, slowly lowering my hands. 'That's what she said her doll was called.'

His eyes still pointed in my direction, but Billy was no longer looking at me. His stare had drifted past me, through the wall at my back, and off into a distant memory.

'But I never told... How did...?' He gave his head a shake and refocused on me. 'How do you know that name?'

'There's no time to explain,' I told him. 'But when I said I met her, I wasn't lying.'

He opened his mouth to interrupt, but I didn't let him. 'I know it's hard to believe, but something happened to me at Christmas. Mr Mumbles, my invisible friend, he came back. He... I don't know how exactly, but he came back.'

Billy blinked. 'Right. It all makes sense now,' he nodded. 'You're mental as well.'

'I thought so too, but it happened, I swear. He came back. He came back and he tried to kill me, and I think it's happening again, only this time it's *your* invisible friend, not mine.'

'I told you, I didn't have—'

'*We don't have time for this,*' I bellowed. The volume of my voice startled us both. I glanced along the corridor to make sure it was still empty, and continued more quietly: 'You had an imaginary friend called Caddie. Little girl, white dress, too much make-up. Caddie owned a doll she called Raggy Maggie. Its body was made of rags, but it had one of those horrible porcelain faces. I know it all, Billy.'

Billy stood, silent.

'I know it's all hard to swallow,' I said, 'but you've got to trust me. If we don't get out of here now, something bad is going to happen.'

When at last Billy spoke, his voice was low and hoarse. 'Like what?'

'Here I come, ready or not.' The voice floated along the

corridor towards us. We both turned in time to see Mrs Milton step round the corner, the scissors still clutched tightly in her right hand. 'Not my fault if you get caught!'

'Like *that*.'

I bolted in the opposite direction, heading for the gloss-painted door that led out into the car park. Billy hesitated, unable to tear his eyes from Mrs Milton, who had begun to skip slowly towards us.

'Come on,' I urged, and at last he began to follow me.

The door rattled in its frame when I turned the handle. Locked. I put a shoulder to it. It shook, but it didn't open.

'Shift over!'

I stepped aside just before Billy's size ten trainer thudded against the door. Again it shook. Again it didn't open.

'Run rabbit, run rabbit, run, run, run.' Mrs Milton was close – *too* close. No time to break the door. No time for anything.

'The gym,' I cried. 'The fire exit.'

'Move then!' All Billy's bravado had slipped away now. He looked as scared as I felt – maybe even more so – as we crashed across the corridor and through the doors of the gym hall.

The gym was the single biggest room in the school. Once a week it doubled as an assembly hall, where we all sat freezing to death and listening to someone drone on about Jesus. It was in sports mode now – the multi-purpose goals had been put up, and the smell of fresh sweat hung heavy in the air.

Over near the middle of the hall, a cream leather football rocked gently from side to side, before gradually coming to rest.

'Where is everyone?' asked Billy. His voice carried across the empty hall like a foghorn.

There should have been a class in here. There *had* been a class in here. I'd heard them. An uneasiness gripped me, but I said nothing. Instead I hurried across the hall to where the emergency exit led out on to the playing field and pushed down on the metal bar.

Thunk. The handle bent all the way down, but the doors remained stuck fast. I pulled the bar up and forced it down again. The result was the same.

'It's locked,' Billy groaned. 'You *idiot*. This was your idea.'

'It's a fire door, it doesn't lock,' I hissed, but there was no arguing with the fact the thing wouldn't budge.

Giving up, I turned and studied the hall. It was a draughty cavern, with high ceilings and a wooden floor that must once have shone with polish, but which now looked scuffed and tired.

There were two exits – the one we'd come through and the one that was stopping us leaving. If we went back out the way we'd entered we would run right into Mrs Milton. If we stayed where we were, she'd run right into us.

'We're trapped,' Billy gasped, taking the words right out of my mouth.

'We have to hide,' I decided. There was a deep alcove at the back of the hall where the sports equipment and assembly chairs were stacked when not in use. It was a blindingly obvious hiding place, but it was the only one we had.

From out in the corridor the *shnick-shnick-shnick* of scissors sliced through the silence. 'She's coming,' I whispered, scurrying across to the alcove. 'Hurry up.'

'We could rush her,' Billy suggested. 'We could knock her out. The two of us.'

'We could,' I admitted, squeezing myself between two towers of stacked wooden chairs. 'But we could also get stabbed in the face.'

'Chicken,' Billy sneered, but he quickly wedged himself into the recess and squatted down beside me.

It was dark there in the alcove – the sloped roof above

us blocking out almost all of the light from the hall's high windows. To begin with the only sound was our own unsteady breathing, until a low *creak* told us the door to the gym hall had been pushed open.

She was singing as she skipped into the hall, letting the door clatter shut behind her. It was below her breath, and too quiet for me to make out the words, but she was definitely whispering some tune or other in that childishly high voice. It set my teeth on edge, like fingernails down a blackboard.

Her voice grew louder as she drew closer to our hiding place. I felt Billy tense up beside me, and realised I was doing the same: rising on to my toes, getting ready to move.

Through the gaps in the chairs I saw her. I bit down on my lip to stop myself crying out in shock. She was just a few feet away, standing right outside the alcove, bent at the waist, peering in.

The song she was singing trailed away into silence as she stared into the darkness. For a moment I was sure she was looking directly at me, and then, in an instant, she straightened up and skipped away.

We held our breath in the gloom, listening as her singing restarted; listening as her feet squeaked on the wooden floor; listening as the door gave another creak and a clatter.

For a few long moments neither of us moved, hardly daring to believe she had gone. It was Billy who eventually broke the silence.

'I think I just crapped my pants.'

It was the last thing I ever expected to hear him say, and I couldn't help but burst out laughing – probably with relief more than anything. My eyes were getting used to the dim light, and I could see that he too was grinning.

'Oh, was that you?' I sniffed. 'I thought it might have been me.'

'Let's get out of here,' he said, and we both stood up. He edged away, making room for me to pass. 'You first.'

'Chicken,' I scoffed, pushing through the gap in the chairs and out into the hall. 'I can't believe she didn't see—'

'Peek-a-boo,' chorused a voice to my left. I spun to find Mrs Milton standing there, just beyond the alcove. Her empty eyes were locked on mine. 'I see you.'

I tried to shout, to scream, but she didn't give me the chance. Her arms jerked suddenly upwards, and from the corner of my eye I caught a glimpse of a hockey stick. A bomb went off against the side of my head, and an explosion of pain shook my skull.

Somewhere far, far away a child giggled. The world lurched, and I found myself tumbling down

down

down into the still, stifling silence of sleep.

Chapter Five

SOMEWHERE ELSE

It was the pain in my wrists that pulled me back from the abyss, waking me with a gasp. My head reeled and spun like I was riding a roller coaster, and for a panicked few seconds I thought I was about to fly right off the... *seat?*

I looked down, ignoring the wave of nausea it brought on. Sure enough, I was sitting on a chair made of plastic and metal. My hands were pulled behind it, wrists bound tightly together and attached to the chair's rusted frame.

The swelling on my cheek throbbed in protest as I raised my head and looked around. The room I was in was dark, and the darkness – like everything else – was fuzzy around the edges. I closed my eyes tight, blinked a couple of times, and tried again.

My vision cleared a little, but it didn't make it any easier to figure out where I was. It was a large, mostly featureless hall. I could make out a few scattered tables and chairs, but very little else. Most of them were broken, toppled over or both.

The floor was a knee-deep mess of shattered glass, rubble and litter. Here and there the smouldering embers of burned rubbish stood out as spots of orange among the shadows. Thin wisps of smoke curled up from some of them, before the breeze coming in through the many holes in the roof carried them away.

Through the broken beams and shattered slates I could make out a dark, cloudy sky. Occasionally I'd spot a star winking at me through a gap, before the clouds rushed to cover it again.

Night time. How long had I been unconscious?

'Hello?' I said. A cloud of breath rolled out into the chill air beside my voice.

'Hello, Kyle.'

My legs spasmed with fright. The voice had come from right behind me. It wasn't Mrs Milton. In fact, it wasn't a woman at all. It was a male voice, and one I was sure I recognised.

He strolled past my left shoulder and stopped a metre or so in front of me. His hands were behind his back – but just held there, not tied like mine. He wore an expression of vague amusement on his face, as if someone had once told him a joke and he was only now getting it.

'What's the matter?' he asked, his voice deep and rich. 'Cat got your tongue?'

I glanced down at the floor, not answering. I didn't know what to say, and even if I did, I'd be too scared to say it.

'Suit yourself,' he shrugged. I lifted my eyes and watched him pick his way through the debris until he found another usable chair. It was half buried under junk, and it took him a few seconds to dig it out.

He lifted huge chunks of stone away as if they were made of polystyrene, and I couldn't help but be a little bit impressed.

The last few things he shoved aside were flat and wooden with edges that curved upwards. It took me a few moments, but then it clicked. They were trays. Wooden trays. Just like the ones in...

The canteen. I craned my neck and took in the room again. It looked about right. Right size. Right shape.

Wrong world.

I've already mentioned the Darkest Corners, the hellish alternative reality I somehow travelled to on Christmas Day. I hadn't just met Caddie there. I'd also met the man who was now walking back towards me, a chair swinging from one hand.

The man who had sent Mr Mumbles after me.

My dad.

The bits of the Darkest Corners I'd seen were just like the real world, only twisted and corrupted. A church back in our world became a crumbling ruin here. A street back home was overgrown with weeds in this reality.

The school canteen, it seemed, had suffered the same sort of fate.

I glanced back down, pretending I hadn't been watching. I saw my dad's foot sweep away a small pile of what looked suspiciously like bones, then the uneven legs of the chair he'd found plonked down on to the filthy floor.

He straddled the chair, his arms resting on its plastic back. I could feel his eyes on me. I raised my head just a fraction. Sure enough, I immediately met his gaze.

'Well, you did it.' He was grinning from ear to ear, his eyebrows raised high on his forehead. 'I have to admit, I was a little surprised when I found out, but there's no—'

'I know who you are,' I told him.

His eyes twinkled. 'Of course you do. That's why I dropped off the photo. I knew your mother would recognise me.'

This wasn't the reaction I had expected. I'm not sure what reaction I did expect, but this wasn't it. Maybe I thought he'd be so impressed by my deductive powers he'd let me go. It hadn't occurred to me that he had deliberately revealed his identity, although in hindsight it seemed painfully obvious.

'How did I get here?'

'I brought you,' he replied, lightning-fast, as if he'd been anticipating the question. 'You're not the only one who can flit between worlds, you know. How do you think Mumbles got out?'

'You brought him?' I said with a gasp.

'Bingo.' The smile stayed on his face, but a seriousness had now clouded his eyes. 'I half expected you to reappear when you got the photo,' he said. 'Thought maybe you'd come looking for me. But... nope.' He pushed a hand through his untidy black hair. 'Still,' he breathed, 'you did it. You actually did it.'

'Did what?' I grunted.

'*Did what?*' he mimicked. 'You beat him, that's what you did. You beat Mr Mumbles.'

'Oh,' I said. 'That.' I gave the rope around my wrists a tug. 'Why did you tie me up?'

'I didn't,' he frowned, waving his hand dismissively. 'It was the girl. So,' he continued, leaning over the back of the chair, like a kid listening to an exciting bedtime story. 'How did it feel?'

The question surprised me. *How did it feel?* He must've caught my thought, because he continued before I could think of what to say.

'Wait, don't tell me,' he said. 'It felt *incredible*, right? All that power. All that strength. That buzz that can only come from taking another life.'

I didn't like the way he said that last part, and I told him so.

'Well, how else can you paint it?' he asked, still smiling. 'You turned the guy to dust. You murdered him.'

'I did not,' I protested. 'He was going to... he would've...'

'Easy, easy,' he said. 'It was self-defence. Absolutely. You had no other choice. No one's blaming you for what you did, killer.' He spoke the word like it was a term of affection.

'Don't call me that,' I said.

'Why not? It's nothing to be ashamed of. It's what you are. It's what *we* are.'

I opened my mouth to argue, but he pushed on, silencing me.

'Don't tell me you didn't feel it,' he said. 'When that power was buzzing across your skin, don't tell me you weren't tempted just to let it take over completely. Just to see where it took you.'

I hesitated. 'No. I wasn't.'

Dad pulled back and laughed. 'Liar.' He leaned in again and shuffled the chair a few centimetres closer. 'Then why didn't you just stop him?' he asked, still smiling. 'You realised you could do all these things, right? So why kill him? Why not just trap him, or send him away?'

'I... I didn't know how,' I said.

'But you knew how to turn plastic into steel?' he pressed. 'Pull lightning from the air – you could do that – but you couldn't imagine him a pair of handcuffs or a cage?'

'I don't... there was no time to think about it.'

'Exactly, so you acted on instinct. Your one true instinct.' His expression shifted into something close to glee. 'The instinct to *kill*.'

'Shut up.'

'We're the same, you and me,' he said. 'There's a darkness inside us both. You can feel it there, can't you? Lurking. Waiting.'

'Shut up.'

'Why haven't you used it again? Why haven't you let it back out?'

'*Shut up,*' I cried.

'It's a part of you, killer,' he continued eagerly. 'Don't fight it. Feel that electricity tingling through your head. Set it free.'

'Why?' I demanded, pulling against the ropes that bound me to the chair. 'Why should I? Why do you care?'

Dad's face took on a more serious expression. 'Because you're my son,' he said. 'And every father wants to see their child reach its full potential.'

He stood up and took two big paces towards me. I screwed up my eyes, half expecting him to hit me. Instead I felt his big hand ruffle through my hair.

'Don't be scared of it, killer,' he told me. 'Embrace it. Surrender to it. And one day every man, woman and child on Earth will know your name. One day you will make the whole damn world burn.'

He began picking his way across the rubble, heading for a hole in the canteen wall. 'One day,' he called back. 'But not today.'

My dad stopped at the wall and peeked into the darkness that lurked outside. His breath formed huge white clouds in the air, but though he was only wearing jeans and a short-sleeved checked shirt, I didn't once notice him shiver.

I was surprised to see someone else standing at the hole in the wall, waiting for him – a shorter, thinner figure, concealed by a long brown cloak and hood. I'd seen this person on my first visit to the Darkest Corners too. He – or she – had trotted after my dad like a lost puppy, never once speaking or even really acknowledging me much. I wondered how long the stranger in the cloak had been standing there, listening out my conversation.

'You remember how you got here the first time?' Dad asked.

I could recall the events leading up to me arriving in the

Darkest Corners last time, but I didn't know if they were directly connected to me making the jump or not. 'I'm... I'm not sure,' I admitted.

'Well, you'd better remember fast,' he grinned. Keeping his eyes on me, he placed two fingers in his mouth. A sharp whistle split the silence of the canteen. 'And if you do make it back,' he said, 'good luck with your second test. She's a nasty one!'

ThuBOOM.

Before I could reply to him, the whole room was shaken by a sudden sound. Plaster dust fell from the ceiling, floating down like flakes of snow.

ThuBOOM.

The second noise was louder than the first. It vibrated the canteen even more violently. Half a roof beam dropped from the shadows just five or six metres away. The table beneath it disintegrated as the thick wooden support crashed down.

ThuBOOM.

Another thud. It echoed and rumbled like the snarling of a thunder god, and I felt my chair shudder a few centimetres across the floor.

ThuBOOM.

ThuBOOM.

THuBOOM.

'What is it?' I gasped. 'What's making that noise?'

My dad was pressed in next to the wall. The figure in brown was nowhere to be seen. Dad was bent at the waist, looking out through the gap in the brickwork. His neck was angled so his eyes were pointing up towards the sky.

'To be honest I'm not sure what it's called,' he said. 'But it sure looks hungry.'

A sound like the end of the world shattered any chance I had of replying. I looked up in time to see the roof being ripped away as if it were made of paper. The silhouette of an enormous head hung there, glaring down.

The faint moonlight picked out four huge, curved tusks in watery shades of silvery-blue. They jutted from the creature's neck and chin, angled so they were all pointing directly at me.

Something dangled down from its wide jaws. At first I thought it was a length of rope, until it dropped off and splashed down, forming a murky pool near my feet. Saliva. Or something like it, anyway.

Its skin had a dull shine to it, like the scales of a snake. It was dark grey or black, but that may have been just the shadows covering the monster's face. The eyes, in contrast, were two slits of dark pink. As they peered at me, the wide cavern of a mouth opened, revealing teeth that were bigger than me. Chunks of rotting meat hung from between some of them, the aftermath of a hundred grizzly meals.

Hot steam hissed from the creature's flared nostrils. It smelled rancid and sour, and burned the lining of my throat like acid.

I let my eyes flick over to the wall for a fraction of a second. My dad had gone. Slunk away somewhere when no one was looking. No surprise there. Running out on people was becoming a trademark of his.

A creeping tingle inched across my scalp. It moved slowly, as if it was scouting to make sure the area was safe.

I coughed back the stench of the dino-beast's breath and concentrated on the sensation. Above me, a long, snake-like tongue flicked across the monstrous teeth. A sound that was somewhere between a yawn and a growl slithered from within the black hole of the creature's throat.

The tingling became a crackle. It arced across my skull, flashing sparks of blue behind my eyes.

The ropes were tight against my wrists. The chair beneath me was hard and uncomfortable. The jaws of death dangled wide and hungry above my head. I blocked it all out and concentrated on the glowing sparks. They surged across my vision at lightning speed. Flash, flash,

flash they went, flecks of white and blue all racing through my head.

The walls of the canteen groaned as the beast leaned down towards me. The heat and stench from its breath were almost unbearable.

Flash. Flash. Flash.

I heard its jaws click as they opened wider.

Flash. Flash. Flash.

Thick strands of drool dribbled on to my legs, coating them in hot, smelly liquid.

The sparks flashed faster and faster. Inside my head I waited. Waited for the right moment. Waited for the right one.

Flash.

Like a jar around a firefly my mind snapped shut on the very next spark. It buzzed furiously, but I held it in place, just as I'd done in the church on Christmas Day.

The world around me began to shimmer and change. I

was doing it. *I was doing it.*

But was I doing it quickly enough?

I glanced up in time to see the dino-beast lunge. Its head came down fast. The pale moonlight glinted briefly off its teeth, and an impossibly large set of jaws snapped sharply shut around me.

Chapter Six

TEA FOR THREE

I screamed, screwing my eyes tight as the teeth cut through the air on either side of my body.

A few seconds later, when no pain came, I cautiously opened my eyes – one first, then the other.

I was in the canteen. The real canteen. I was still tied to a chair, and the bruising on my face still hurt like hell, but I'd done it. I'd brought myself back.

I looked around at the room. It was bright and clean – well, cleaner than the place I'd just left, at least. Daylight shone through the windows. A half-sigh, half-sob of relief escaped my lips. It was good to be back.

As I studied my surroundings, I noticed my chair was now positioned right next to one of the canteen's big round dining tables. Small, floral-patterned cups and saucers had been laid out in three places – one in front of me, one directly across the table, and the third halfway between those two. Another chair had been positioned at the placing across from me, but not at the one on my right.

A sugar bowl and a milk jug sat on the table too. Like the cups, both of these were empty.

From over my left shoulder I heard a whimper. By craning my neck as far as it would go, I could make out the shape of someone lying on the floor.

Mrs Milton was curled up into a ball, her knees almost to her chest, her arms clutching her head. Her whole body was shaking. Every few seconds it would twitch wildly, forcing another whimper from her trembling lips.

'Mrs Milton?' I said. Although I spoke softly, the sound still made my skull throb. She didn't respond, so I tried again. 'Mrs Milton, are you OK?'

'She doesn't want to play with us any more.'

I froze. The voice was the same one the headmistress had used – or maybe *it* had been using *her* – but it hadn't come out of her mouth. It had come from somewhere further behind me, beyond my line of sight.

I recognised the voice right away as the one I'd heard during my first visit to the Darkest Corners.

'Caddie.'

The little girl in the dirty white dress stepped into my line of sight. 'Oh, you remembered,' she beamed. As she did, the bright line of lipstick across her mouth curved into an exaggerated smile, like the grin of some demented clown.

'What did you do to her?' I demanded.

Caddie's face fell. Her wide, dark eyes blinked rapidly, as if fighting back tears. 'She won't play any more,' she said. 'We were having so much fun, but then she just wouldn't play.'

Down on my left, the headmistress gave another low sob. 'S'not fair,' Caddie sulked. 'Every time I find a new friend to play with they get broken.'

I twisted in my seat and looked down at Mrs Milton. She was rocking back and forth, weeping, shaking – a shadow of the woman she had been. Bruised. Battered.

Broken.

When I turned back, Caddie was standing by the table. Her back was to me and she was fiddling with something on the tabletop. The way she was bending her body made it impossible for me to see what.

'Where's Billy?' I asked.

'Not telling.'

'What have you done with him?'

'I told you, silly,' she giggled, turning back to face me. 'I'm not telling!'

She skipped past and disappeared behind me, leaving me alone with the thing she'd been positioning on the table.

The porcelain face of the doll was slumped sideways on the bundle of grubby material that made up its body. A long dark crack ran from the top of its head and down the left side of its face, completely obscuring one eye. The other eye squinted across the table at me, painted on, but eerily lifelike.

Raggy Maggie had seemed disturbing enough in the Darkest Corners, but here in the school the doll was somehow even more chilling.

'Tea?'

I jumped in my seat as Caddie appeared beside me. She was holding a small plastic teapot. Her wide eyes looked at me expectantly.

'What?' I spluttered. 'No.'

Immediately her face darkened, as if a shadow had crawled across it. 'But it's a tea party,' she glowered. 'Why would you come to a tea party if you weren't going to have tea?'

I glanced from Caddie to the doll on the table. Its single eye bored into me, as if waiting for my answer.

'Go on then,' I croaked, turning back to the little girl. Her face brightened at once. 'Just a small one.'

'Oh, goody,' she trilled. 'Maybe if you're *extra* good you might even get a cake.'

I nodded nervously. 'Yum.'

Maybe you're wondering why I was so scared of a girl with a doll. If so then you've obviously never met Caddie. If you had, you'd know *exactly* why I was playing along with her little tea party scene.

As soon as I'd set eyes on her in the Darkest Corners, I could tell there was something 'wrong' about Caddie. At first glance she looked more or less like any other five-year-old girl, but it didn't take long to realise she was something much more sinister than that.

Partly it was her eyes – the irises almost filled them, so dark as to be virtually black, like two gaping holes in her head. The make-up didn't help, either: dark blue circles ringing the eyes, a crimson smear across the lips and a smudge of red on each pale cheek.

The words she said could have been those of any other kid her age, but the way she spoke implied a deeper, darker meaning behind them that only she was aware of. She also had a strange intensity about her, as if she were three wrong words away from becoming very, very angry. Somehow I knew that making her very, very angry would be a very, very stupid thing to do.

Caddie was, in short, more frightening than any little girl had any right to be. And as for the doll... Don't get me started on the doll.

Caddie hummed below her breath as she tipped the spout of her teapot over my cup. Nothing came out, but this didn't seem to bother her in the slightest.

'Sugar?' she asked, when she'd finished pouring.

'No,' I said. 'Thanks.'

She frowned briefly, but said nothing, and carried on round the table to where Raggy Maggie was slumped. Once again she tipped the contents of her toy teapot into the waiting cup. 'Raggy Maggie likes sugar, don't you, Raggy Maggie?'

The doll, as expected, didn't reply.

After spooning some invisible sugar and pouring some imaginary milk into her doll's cup, Caddie moved around to the opposite side of the table and took her seat. She was so short she had to stretch up in the chair to pour her own pretend tea. Milk. Eight sugars.

'Drink up,' she giggled. She took a sip from her own cup. The *shlurp* sound she made was surprisingly convincing. 'Oh, I forgot,' she said, smiling, 'you can't. You're all tied up.'

'What do you want?' I asked.

Shlurp. 'Mmm, a biscuit would be nice. A chocolate one. With sprinkles.'

'No, I mean... *what do you want?*'

She sat her cup down on the saucer. Those dark, empty eyes of hers fixed firmly on me. I could feel the doll staring at me too, but I tried not to think about it.

'Just to play,' she said with an exaggerated shrug. 'We just want to have fun, that's all. Nothing's fun where we live.'

'The Darkest Corners.'

Her face changed in an instant. Her eyes narrowed, pushed down by her eyebrows as her mouth pulled into an angry snarl. 'Don't you say that,' she cried. 'Don't say that place!'

She was on her feet before I knew it, snatching up her cup. She thrust it sharply forward, as if throwing her imaginary tea. I almost smiled, before the pain hit me.

Nothing had been poured into the cup, and I saw nothing come out of it, but as soon as she'd chucked it towards me a blisteringly hot liquid hit the top of my school jumper and began to soak through my shirt.

I let out a hiss of shock as the skin on my chest began to burn. Caddie continued to glare. I knew she wasn't going to help me. No one was. I had no choice but to screw my eyes shut, grit my teeth and wait for the pain to pass.

The worst of it probably faded in less than a minute, although it felt like longer. In just a few minutes more I was left with merely a dull ache, although it was made worse by the fact that my shirt was clinging to it.

Caddie was still standing up on the other side of the table, but her face was no longer twisted so fiercely. She gave a little cough as she lowered herself back into her seat and poured another cup of boiling hot nothing.

'That was your fault,' she explained. Her voice was back to normal again, all trace of the rage that had gripped her gone. 'I didn't want to do that, but you made...'

Her voice trailed off and she turned to look at her doll.

'What's that, Raggy Maggie?' she asked, reaching over and carefully lifting the bundle of rags off the table.

She held the doll to her ear, moving its head up and down slightly, as if it was whispering to her. For a moment I almost wondered what it was saying, until I reminded myself it was only a toy.

'Hmm, I don't know, Raggy Maggie,' Caddie murmured. Her eyes were still on me, not blinking. 'You think we should do *what* to him?'

I watched the scene playing out before me, barely aware that I was holding my breath. My hands wriggled at my back as I struggled to free them from the rope or wire or whatever it was that was holding them together.

It was no use. The harder I struggled, the deeper my bonds dug into my wrists. All I could do was sit there. Sit there and wait to find out what Caddie had in store.

'Oh, but he's a *nice* boy,' Caddie protested. 'He might be our friend.' The doll's head waggled up and down more forcefully. 'He didn't know they were bad words,' the girl continued. 'It's not fair!'

Raggy Maggie stopped moving – just for a moment – then gave a final few nods of her head.

'OK,' Caddie nodded, her face brightening. She turned her wrist so the doll's solitary eye was looking towards me. 'Raggy Maggie wants you to say sorry for saying the bad words,' the girl explained. 'I think you'd better. She's very cross.'

My lips had gone dry. I licked them, but there was no saliva left in my mouth, so it didn't help. 'Sorry,' I croaked.

'Say it properly.' Caddie stood up and stretched across the table, holding out the doll so its expressionless face was just a few centimetres from my own. Up close it smelled sour, like a carton of milk a month past its sell-by-date.

'Sorry for saying the bad words,' I said. I felt like an idiot, but more than anything I wanted the doll out of my face.

'Thank you for being so nice, Raggy Maggie,' prompted Caddie.

I hesitated, but then carried on. 'Thanks for being so nice.'

Raggy Maggie's porcelain head bobbed up and down. As it did, Caddie spoke in a harsh, scratchy voice. 'You're welcome,' the voice said. 'Don't do it again.'

The doll was pulled back across the table, but wasn't put down in its place. Instead Caddie held on to it, both of them facing me. We sat there in silence for a long time, the occasional whimper from Mrs Milton the only sound to be heard.

I was about to say something – anything – when Caddie spoke. 'We're going to play a game,' she told me, her eyes sparkling with excitement. My heart sank. The groans from the headmistress testified to the damage Caddie's games could do.

'What kind of game?'

'A *fun* game. It's like hide-and-seek, only *better*!' She was bouncing up and down in her seat now, barely containing her delight. 'Me and Raggy Maggie will go and hide somewhere, and you've got to find us.'

'OK...' I said, hardly believing my luck. Once they were out of the way I could find a way to get free and escape. 'Sounds good.'

'I'm not finished yet, silly,' Caddie giggled. 'Because we're not going to be hiding all by ourselves. We're going to be hiding with our best friend in the whole wide world.' She hugged Raggy Maggie tightly to her face. 'Billy.'

That complicated things a bit, but not much. I would still go and get help. Yes, Billy might be stuck with Little Miss Crazy and her dolly for a while, but he'd made my life a misery for years, and I found it difficult to feel too bad for him.

'And here's the best part of all,' Caddie gushed. 'We'll

all be hiding somewhere here in the school, and if you don't find us in one hour...' She glanced at her doll and giggled. 'Billy *dies*.'

Chapter Seven

THE GAME BEGINS

"**F**our little rules,' continued Caddie, barely pausing for breath after dropping her bombshell. 'One, you're not allowed to leave the school. Go outside and something bad happens to Billy.'

'Something bad like what?'

Caddie shrugged. 'Up to Raggy Maggie. She's good at doing bad things.'

I nodded. 'I bet. What's the second rule?'

'No shouting for help,' Caddie warned. 'If we catch you doing that, something bad happens to Billy. Something even *worse* than bad.'

'Got it,' I said.

'Rule number C is that you're not allowed to use your magic powers. We know all about them, and if you use them even once then that's cheating.'

'What'll happen if I do?'

'Something bad, of course!' Caddie giggled. 'How many rules is that?'

'Three.'

'OK. Rule number four is the most important of all, so listen very carefully.' She got up from her chair and skipped round to where I was sitting, swinging Raggy Maggie by her arms.

When she reached me, she rested a hand on my shoulder. Her dark eyes stared into mine, her face solemn and sincere. 'The most important rule of all,' she said, quietly, 'is: have fun.' Her face broke into a broad, happy smile. 'Winning's not important.'

'It's pretty important for Billy,' I pointed out.

'Well, yes, but it's the taking part that counts. If a game's not fun, then what's the point in playing it?'

'Right,' I said. 'Have fun. I'll try.'

'Oh, goodie!' she beamed. 'Any questions?'

'Just one. What makes you think I'll play?' I asked. 'I don't even like Billy. What makes you think I'll help him?'

'Because Daddy said you would,' Caddie replied. 'He says you'd want to play at being the big brave hero.'

I frowned. 'What? I don't even know who your dad is.'

'Not *my* daddy, silly.'

She turned away and looked up at the wall behind me. Her lips moved as she silently tried to work something out in her head. 'What's it called when the big hand is at twelve and the little hand is at two?' she asked.

'Two o'clock.'

'And what's one hour up from two o'clock?'

'Four o'clock,' I said, hoping to buy myself some more time.

'Liar, liar, pants on fire,' she sang. Her hand reached for the teapot on the table. I closed my eyes and braced myself for the pain.

A howl of anguish rose up from Mrs Milton. I opened my eyes and whipped my head round. Caddie was standing behind me, tipping the teapot over the head teacher. As before there was nothing to be seen coming from the spout, but Mrs Milton was thrashing around in pain, babbling and sobbing as her skin blistered and burned.

'Stop it,' I pleaded. 'Stop it, leave her alone.'

'Cheating is very naughty,' Caddie tutted, tipping the teapot up to empty the last of the contents over the helpless headmistress. 'This is what happens when you cheat.'

'But it was me who cheated, not her. It's me you should be punishing.'

Caddie stopped pouring and gave that little high-pitched giggle again. 'See? Daddy was right,' she said. Opening the lid of the teapot, she peeked inside. 'All done,' she shrugged, and she let it drop to the floor.

I watched Mrs Milton lie there, still writhing in pain. I've never felt more guilty for anything in my whole life.

'Three o'clock, don't be late,' Caddie said, slipping her feet back into her oversized shoes. 'Billy's counting on it.'

'Are you going to untie me?'

'Don't be silly, that's part of the game.' She skipped her way towards the canteen door. Halfway there she stopped and listened to the whispers of her doll. 'Oh yes, you're right, Raggy Maggie, I nearly forgot.'

She turned back and flashed me another smile. 'I brought some other friends to play too. You'll have to get past them if you're going to find us.' Something menacing glinted behind her eyes. 'Don't worry, they're lots and lots of fun.'

With one final giggle, she skipped on out of the canteen, leaving me alone with the wreckage of my head teacher.

'It's OK, Mrs Milton, I'm going to get us out of here,' I promised, although I didn't yet know how I was going to manage it. Whatever Caddie had used to tie my wrists was stronger than I was. No matter how hard I pulled I couldn't get free. For a five-year-old, the girl could tie a serious knot.

From the corner of my eye I saw something move over by one of the canteen's tall, narrow windows. A long green curtain fluttered as it was pushed aside, and a short little man popped his balding head out.

'She gone?' he asked.

I nodded. The man seemed to relax at this, and he stepped out from behind the curtain.

'Twice I nearly sneezed back there,' he said, blowing out his cheeks. 'Dust in the 'tache.' He gave his greying moustache a brush with his fingertips. 'Can you imagine if I had? Disaster.'

'You were there the whole time?' I scowled. 'You just hid there and didn't do anything to stop her?'

'*Stop* her?' the man snorted. 'How am *I* supposed to stop *her*?'

'Let me see. Maybe because she's a little girl and you're a sixty-year-old man?'

The man's face lit up. 'Sixty? Really? Sixty years old? Me?' He shook his head in delighted disbelief. 'Sixty. That's made my day, that has. I'm actually sixty-seven.'

'I don't care,' I hissed, as he took a few steps closer. 'I still don't... Hey, wait a minute, don't I know you?'

Now I could see him properly, there was something very familiar about the man. The balding head. The moustache. The sagging jaw and podgy belly. I'd seen him before, but where?

'We've met,' he nodded. 'You wouldn't pull my cracker with me.'

'You're that policeman,' I gasped. 'From the station.'

Ameena and I had taken sanctuary in the police station when we were running from Mr Mumbles. Although he didn't seem to believe me when I told him we were being chased, the policeman had finally agreed to go outside and see if he could spot anyone acting suspiciously.

A few minutes later he'd come crashing through the door. I could still remember the noise he'd made as he struck the back wall. The sight and smell of his blood was as vivid now as it had been back then. I'd gone back to try to find him, but by the time I returned he had vanished. I had no idea what had happened to him until now.

'I thought you were dead,' I told him.

'I just wished I was,' he said, wincing at the memory. 'For a while, at least. Being thrown head-first through a double-glazed door does that to you.'

He crossed to Mrs Milton and knelt by her. I couldn't see his face from my seat, but the way he sucked his breath in through his teeth told me he was worried.

'Will she be OK?'

'Hard to say,' he replied. 'Caddie's hurt her pretty

badly. Scrambled her brain right up.'

I paused for a moment, replaying the last couple of sentences in my head, making sure I'd heard him correctly. When I was confident that I had I asked, 'How do you know her name?'

He turned, still crouching, and looked up at me. 'Because I'm not really a policeman, Kyle,' he said. I opened my mouth to ask more, but he silenced me with a wave of his hand. 'No time for that now. You've got to find the boy before it's too late.'

'Billy!' I exclaimed. I'd almost forgotten.

The man gestured down at Mrs Milton. She was still just lying there. Still sobbing. Still broken. 'I can help you,' he began, 'or I can help her. Your choice.'

'Help her,' I said quickly, in case I changed my mind.

He nodded, then began to untie the ropes binding me. 'She's not alone. She's brought... others,' he warned. 'And don't believe anything she tells you. You can't trust her, so be careful.'

The tightness on my wrists loosened and I felt the blood begin to rush back into my tingling hands.

'I will,' I said, standing up. My head still ached from where the hockey stick had smacked into it, but I ignored it as best I could.

'One quick question,' the man began. I turned and looked down at him.

'What?'

'Your... abilities. You didn't use them to get free. Why?'

'How did you know about—?'

'Tell you later. Why didn't you?'

I hesitated, not quite sure how to explain it. 'Because... I can't. I haven't been able to do anything. Not since... since I did those things. On the roof.'

That wasn't quite the truth. The truth was I'd been too scared even to try. What my dad had said had only confirmed what I'd suspected since Christmas. The power inside me felt dangerous. I was frightened by it. Every time I'd felt it flicker I'd pushed it back down as quickly as I could.

'I see,' he said, nodding his head. 'Well, you heard her rules – don't start using them now. If she says something bad will happen, you don't want to be the one it happens to.' He glanced at his watch. 'Now, time's running out. Go find that boy.'

'Right,' I agreed, heading for the door through which Caddie had left. Just before I reached it, I turned back. 'I didn't even get your name,' I said, before realising that neither the man nor Mrs Milton were anywhere in the canteen.

I crept out into the corridor, a little weirded out by the man's sudden disappearance. He was the second person to pull a vanishing act on me today, not including Billy, who probably hadn't had much in the way of choice.

According to the clock on the corridor wall it was already ten past two. That meant I had fifty minutes to find Billy. It also meant the school should be bustling with pupils on their way to their final classes of the day, but there wasn't another soul in sight.

The canteen corridor opened out into a wide hall area, off which ran half a dozen doors. The caretaker's office was here, as well as a storeroom, some classrooms and a final glass door that led to a set of wide stairs.

The door to the caretaker's tiny windowless room was open, but there was no sign of life inside. I listened at each of the classroom doors in turn, but heard nothing from within any of those, either.

Cautiously I turned the brass handle on one of the doors. It inched open without a sound, and I poked my head inside the classroom.

Textbooks lay open on every desk. Bags and coats hung

over the backs of chairs.

'Hello?' I ventured, pushing the door further open and stepping into the room. No one replied, but then there was nobody there *to* reply.

I'd never been in this class before, but I was vaguely aware of seeing it full of older kids with tufty goatee beards, who looked older than some of the teachers. A glance at a workbook on the closest desk confirmed this. The open page displayed an English essay that made almost no sense to me.

Two-thirds of the way down the page the essay came to an abrupt, sudden stop. Halfway through a sentence it just ended, mid-word.

The writer had left their pen sitting next to the book. A quick look round the room revealed a pen either on top of each desk, or on the floor directly beneath them. Wherever the class had gone, they'd gone there in a hurry.

Except none of the chairs had been disturbed. They

were all pulled in close to the desks, but not tucked under them. Either the students had partially pushed their seats back under the desks after standing up, or... no. I dismissed the idea. It was impossible. They *couldn't* have.

An entire class couldn't just vanish into thin air.

Still, the thought haunted me, and I felt a sudden urge to get out of the room. Besides, time was ticking away. I had only forty-five minutes to find Billy, and a whole lot of school to cover.

The hall was still empty when I left the class. I realised that no matter where I'd been in the school in the past there had always been some kind of noise. Pupils talking. Teachers shouting. The caretaker whistling. Always some kind of background soundtrack. Always something to be heard. Always.

But not now.

Now there was only silence, heavy and ominous. The calm before the storm.

I didn't look in any of the other classes around the hall. I was sure they'd be pretty much identical to the one I'd just been in. Besides, I didn't think Caddie would hide Billy so close.

So where *would* she hide him? The school had dozens of rooms – probably sixty at the very least – not to mention all the little nooks and crannies that filled its many corners. He could be anywhere. I didn't even know where to start.

At least, I didn't until I saw the sign.

The glass-panelled door that led to the stairs squeaked sharply as I edged it open and stepped through. I was too busy staring to hear it bang shut again behind me.

Fifteen stairs led up from where I was standing. They stopped at a little rectangular landing, before fifteen more steps doubled back in the opposite direction and continued upwards to the first floor.

A huge image – easily one-and-a-bit times my size – had been smeared on the wall of the halfway turning point. A thick, red liquid had been used to paint the picture. It trickled and dribbled down the wall, forming dark crimson pools on the scuffed lino floor.

I didn't want to believe it, but I knew the liquid was blood. *Lots* of blood, forming the shape of an arrow.

An arrow pointing up.

Chapter Eight

SHADOWS OF THE LOST

There was a stale, coppery tint to the air as I edged past the halfway landing and crept on up the stairs. The arrow towered over me, slowly dribbling down the wall, painting it with streaks of glistening red.

I tried to dodge past the puddles of blood, but there was no way to avoid them completely. I tried to concentrate on what lay ahead, but it was hard not to think about the squelching of my feet, or the sticky crimson footprints that followed me up to the first floor.

Another arrow – smaller, but just as disturbing – had been smeared on to the wall here too. This time, though, the arrow wasn't pointing up. Instead it was pointing along one of the two corridors that ran off at right angles from the stairway. The art corridor. Of course. I should have guessed.

It's probably a good idea if I explain how the school is laid out, otherwise things might get a bit confusing.

Basically, if you were to be peering down on the building from above, it'd look like the outline of a big square. All four sides are exactly five classrooms long, and each side is three floors high, not including the ground one.

At every corner there is a set of stairs, identical to the ones I'd just walked up. They're designed to be wide enough to let traffic move up and down at the same time, but more often than not it's a running battle to try to get to wherever you're going, with everyone pushing in every direction at once.

Each floor is painted a different colour. With the layout of every level being almost exactly the same, doing them all in different colours was probably the only way of making sure anyone could figure out where they were. Either that or no one could decide on a colour scheme.

The first floor – where I was now – was mostly pale blue. It housed the music corridor, two language corridors and the art corridor. It was this last one that the arrow dripping down the wall was pointing to. This was not good news.

The art corridor is unique in the school in that it is the only one that doesn't fit the colour pattern. Three of the corridors on the first floor are the pale blue I mentioned, but the art corridor isn't. The art corridor just had to be different.

At some point in the dim and distant past, someone had decided to decorate the art corridor with a series of random murals. Judging by the results, they'd given a load of paint, rollers and brushes to the least artistically able pupils they could find, and left them to go mental.

It looked truly awful. Every available surface had been

covered, not just the walls. There were paintings on the floor, paintings on the doors – even the ceiling hadn't survived unscathed, though what the picture up there was supposed to be was anyone's guess.

Most significantly, given my current situation, some bright spark had decided to paint over the windows – right on to the glass itself. Not only did this look rubbish, it also more or less blocked out all the daylight that should have been coming in from outside. This meant the whole multicoloured mess was lit by just four low-powered fluorescent strips.

It was the darkest corridor in the whole school, and there was an arrow painted in blood pointing along it. It had to be a trap. Going that way would be insane. Maybe even suicide. Unfortunately time was ticking away, and I didn't have a whole lot of choice.

Steeling myself, I set off, eyes peeled for anything out of the ordinary. The overhead lights were doing their job, and

I could see right to the far end of the corridor where the stairs led up to the second floor.

The temptation to run to the other end was almost overwhelming, but running carried its own risks. Running meant I might not see trouble coming until it was too late. I could just as easily be running into danger as running away from it.

So instead I walked slowly along the corridor, my eyes darting at shadows every step of the way. I wasn't sure what kind of 'friends' Caddie had been talking about, but I was certain I didn't want to bump into any of them.

As I passed the first few doors I realised they were closed. Normally the classrooms were only closed when a lesson was in progress. Even though the doors were shut now, there was nothing but silence behind them, and I found myself wondering once again where everyone was.

They *could* have all left when I was in the Darkest Corners, but I didn't know why they would. A fire alarm, possibly? But then where were the fire engines? And one of the assembly points was right outside the canteen. No one had been lined up there. I'd have seen them.

Besides, I couldn't shake the feeling everyone had left before then. Morag hadn't been at her usual place in the reception area, and the whole school had seemed strangely still and silent when I'd escaped from Mrs Milton's office with Billy.

Billy. Dislike him as I did, I still found myself worrying about him, which annoyed me a little. I'd had enough sense not to provoke Caddie too much, but I wasn't so sure Billy would be able to do the same. By his very nature he was incredibly irritating. If he said the wrong thing to Caddie there was no saying what she would do to him.

I had to find him. I had to save him. As I continued down the corridor, though, I wondered whether he'd even appreciate it if I did. If we swapped places, I don't expect for one minute he'd even attempt to rescue me.

Around a third of the way along, the hairs on my arm suddenly stood on end, and my skin puckered into tiny goosebumps. A shiver travelled the length of my spine. From nowhere a cold breeze tingled at the nape of my neck. Deep down in my stomach something primal tensed, warning me that I was being watched.

Still walking, I glanced back over my shoulder. For the tiniest fraction of a second I thought I saw something move across the floor. A shadow, maybe; there one moment, gone the next.

A trick of the light, that was all. Had to be. The corridor was empty in both directions. There was nobody here but me.

Nevertheless, I felt my pace quicken and my heartbeat race to keep up. I was halfway along the corridor now. It felt too narrow, claustrophobic; closing in. I couldn't wait to be out of it.

Just a few seconds, I told myself, fighting to ignore the

rising feeling of panic in my gut. I glanced back again, and this time saw something vaguely spider-like moving across the floor and up the wall. A shadow. Definitely a shadow.

But a shadow of what?

I broke into a fast jog, scanning the corridor behind me for any more signs of life. Nothing moved. Nothing scuttled. Nothing there.

I turned and faced ahead just in time to see a dark shape step out of the final classroom and directly into my path.

My arms flailed as I back-pedalled wildly, trying to stop before I crashed into the looming figure. I cursed myself for getting spooked into running. I was going to run right into them. *Stupid, stupid, stupid.*

'There you are,' said the girl blocking my way. 'Been looking for you everywhere.'

'Ameena?' I wheezed, managing to bring my run to a stumbling end right in front of her. I was so relieved I almost cheered. 'It's you! I thought you were... something horrible.'

'Oh. Thanks for that,' she replied, raising her thin eyebrows. 'Very nice of you to say so.'

'No,' I said, hurriedly explaining. 'I saw... I mean, I *thought I saw* something behind me, and...' Her puzzled, vaguely amused expression suddenly made me feel like an idiot and I let the sentence fall away. 'What are you doing here, anyway?'

'Came looking for you,' she shrugged. 'Glad I did,' she said after a pause. 'You look kind of freaked out.' Her eyes fell on the black and blue splodge on my cheek. 'And what happened to your face?'

'Headmistress with a hockey stick, but I'm fine.' I took a breath, preparing to tell her it all. Billy. Mrs Milton. Caddie. Every detail.

Before I could, the overhead lights dimmed to a dull glow, plunging the corridor into near darkness. 'OK, *now*

I'm freaked out,' I admitted. 'Come on. Let's get out of here.'

I moved to go past her, but she caught me by the arm. Her grip was strong – much stronger than I'd expected.

'Why, what's going on?' she demanded. She peered through the gloom behind me. 'What did you see back there?'

'Just shadows.' I tried to pull my arm away, but she had it held tight. Her eyes bored into me, searching for answers. 'Look, I'll explain everything,' I promised, 'but can we please get out of the dark first?'

Her grip relaxed and I took my arm back. 'Fine,' she said. 'But stop getting so freaked out. What kind of superhero gets scared by his own shadow?'

I was halfway through telling her I was no superhero when the darkness took her. It unfurled from the wall at her back, like a giant bat opening its leathery wings. In an instant it had snapped shut. Swallowing her. Devouring her whole.

The black shape that had been Ameena writhed and thrashed furiously. I could only watch, numb with shock, too stunned to help her. All around us, warped, deformed shadows began to skulk across the walls, across the floor, across the ceiling and the doors and the poorly painted windows.

Vicious, brutal shapes, they were. Spiders. Wolves. Flapping bats. Demented, demonic shadow puppets, seeping from the woodwork until every surface of the corridor moved and ebbed. A tide of pure liquid black.

At either end of the corridor the darkness on the ceiling poured down to meet the darkness on the floor. It hung there at either end, two curtains of night, cutting off any chance of escape.

A muffled scream from Ameena snapped me out of my daze. I sprang forward, ripping and clawing at the shadows that smothered her. They were thick and gloopy and cold to the touch. They came away in long stringy threads as I fought to uncover her face.

Her eyes were revealed first. They were bulging and bloodshot, the pupils dilated in terror. I caught the edges of the black sludge and pulled down, fighting to free her nose and mouth. Fighting to keep her alive.

Thick strands of the stuff tore off with an elastic *snap*. I heard Ameena's breath draw in sharply, but the blackness had already flooded back over her eyes. No matter how quickly I ripped it away, any gap I created closed back up almost at once.

'Getitoff, getitoff.' She barely managed to get the words out before her mouth was swallowed up once again.

The strands I'd already torn off had quickly wrapped themselves around my wrists. Even as I fought to free Ameena I could feel them slithering up the insides of my shirt sleeves, cold and clammy against my skin.

Twins bands of the goop squirmed up beneath my collar. For a moment they curled up in front of my face, coiling and wriggling like tentacles, and then they were tight around my throat, cutting off my air.

Frantically I dug my fingers into them, trying to force my nails underneath, to prise them off. No use. Too tight. *Too tight.*

A puddle of chill damp oozed over my shoes. A heaving mass of dark shapes rose from the floor. I watched on helplessly as the darkness began to creep and crawl up my legs.

I was still gasping for air as it passed my knees. Still spluttering as it oozed up over my stomach and chest. Still choking as the shadows wrapped their arms around me, cocooning me and dragging me down into an inky void of absolute black.

Chapter Nine

SWALLOWED WHOLE

I have almost drowned twice in my life. Once was when I was five. The other was two weeks ago. Christmas Day. I don't recommend it. It's a horrible sensation – that feeling of absolute hopelessness and inevitability as your lungs burn like fire and your head goes light and you brace yourself for the end.

This was worse.

The shadows squirmed across my skin and scurried through my hair. They forced through my clenched lips and rushed up my nostrils, flooding my insides with their icy cold touch. They slithered in through my ears and pushed below my eyelids, filling my head with a pulsating cloud of darkness.

They tightened around my body, forcing my arms to my sides. My legs too were pulled together, throwing my balance. I didn't realise I was falling until my shoulder crunched solidly against the floor. The darkness that covered me felt thick and oily, but it didn't do anything to cushion the blow.

As I lay there – trapped, helpless and rapidly running out of air – the electrical sensation tingled across my scalp. It was faint, but it was there. This time I didn't push it away. If I could concentrate, if I could just focus for a few seconds, then maybe I could get out of this.

Then I remembered the third rule. Caddie had said I wasn't allowed to use my abilities. Something bad would happen, she had warned. Then again, something bad was happening now. I couldn't think of anything worse, in fact.

I hesitated. I *could* probably use my power to get us out

of this, but was there another way? Another way that wouldn't break Caddie's rules? Maybe.

The black shroud around me made it impossible to know exactly where I had fallen, but I could take a guess. The windows had been at my left when I'd been standing up, and I'd landed on my right shoulder.

I bucked my body against the writhing shadows, trying desperately to shuffle myself down in the direction of my feet. The pressure was building around me. A tightness like the grip of an icy claw was squeezing at my lungs. If this didn't work then I was dead.

It was going to work. It *had* to work. These things were shadows, and shadows had a weakness.

Through the gloop I felt my heels bump into something solid. Not too solid, I hoped.

Struggling against my bonds I raised both knees to my chest and fired both feet out, aiming as high up as I could manage. The painted windowpane shuddered in its frame.

Again I brought my legs up, and again I powered them towards the glass. Again it failed to break, and the shadows tightened further around me until I felt as if my bones would break under the strain.

Come on, you can do this, I told myself, pulling my knees right up to my chin. With one final thrust I lashed out, forcing the very last of my strength into the kick.

The effect was instantaneous. As the glass smashed the sunlight flooded in. It was weak and watery – January sunlight – but it was enough to make the shadows screech and squeal and thrash around in pain.

They stung my skin as they tore themselves off, retreating away from the window and back into the dark. I wanted to lie there for a moment and get my breath back, but there was no time. Ameena remained motionless on the floor, still bound by the blackness.

My legs moved slowly, as if they were knee-deep in mud, as I pulled myself up. The shadows were all staying back from the light, leaving the floor around me clear to do what I needed to do.

A sideways step. A snapping out of my foot. A shattering of glass, as the next window along exploded outwards. The closest of the shadows evaporated with a hiss in the glow of the sunlight. Those covering Ameena began to pulse uneasily.

Another step. Another kick. Another window. The entire corridor seemed to be howling. A thousand different voices all screaming in unison. It was an inhuman, unholy sound.

I loved it.

With another swing of my leg I shattered the window next to Ameena. The shadows that were wrapped around her exploded into dust, as those close to her fled from the stabbing shards of the daylight.

She wasn't moving; wasn't breathing; wasn't *living*. I dropped to my knees next to her and felt clumsily for a pulse. It was somewhere in the neck, I knew, but where?

It didn't matter. Her normally olive skin looked almost pale blue. Her chest wasn't moving. I had to act fast.

Her head tilted back easily. Tilting the head opened up the airway. I remembered that bit from a first-aid demonstration I'd once seen. Pity I couldn't remember the rest of it.

Was I supposed to pinch her nose? There was definitely something about the nose, but was it *make sure you pinch the nose* or was it *for God's sake, DON'T pinch the nose*? I should have been paying more attention.

'Shut up!' I shouted into the screeching darkness. Its agitated chittering was cutting through me now; a buzzsaw in my skull, making it hard to think.

I decided to pinch the nose. I couldn't see what harm it could do. Her condition couldn't exactly get much worse than 'dead'. There was nowhere to go but up from there.

Her nostrils squeezed flat easily between my thumb and

index finger. I took a deep breath, opened her mouth, and leaned in.

Her eyes flicked wide just before our lips met. I pulled backwards in fright, the air escaping my lungs in a strangled cry of shock.

'What are you doing?' she demanded. 'Were you going to kiss me?'

'What?' I spluttered. '*No!* I was... I mean, not like that! You were dead.'

She propped herself up on to her elbows. 'No I wasn't.'

'Well, you looked dead to me,' I insisted.

'So what, it's OK to kiss someone if they're dead, is it? That's fine as far as you're concerned?'

'It was the kiss of life,' I protested.

Her mouth pulled into a wide, toothy grin. 'Just kidding.'

She sprang to her feet as if nothing had happened to her. I watched her standing there, hands on her hips, studying our surroundings.

The squealing from the shadows had died down to just a few low whines. We were standing in a pool of light, into which the darkness could not seem to spread. It lurked around the edges, though, waiting for its chance to strike.

'Man,' she said with a shake of her head, 'and I thought Mr Mumbles was weird. This is a whole other level.'

I nodded in agreement. 'You're telling me.'

She turned back to me, hands still fixed to her hips. 'So what is it?'

I looked up at the shapes moving on the ceiling. They seemed thinner there, more spaced out. I remembered the first one I'd seen scuttling across the floor and up the wall. Its eight legs had almost looked like long, spindly fingers.

'I think they're sort of... shadow puppets.'

A pause. 'Shadow puppets? You're kidding.'

I shrugged. 'I think that's what they are.'

'Shadow puppets don't smother people,' she retorted. 'Shadow puppets don't force themselves down people's throats. Say what you like about shadow puppets, *they don't try to kill you.*'

'These ones do.'

She'd probably have kept arguing had a thought not suddenly struck her.

'Hey, how did you get out? You do the whole superhero thing again?'

'I broke a window,' I explained. 'And I'm not a superhero.'

'You broke a window? Why didn't you just zap them off, or whatever it is you do?'

'I'm not allowed. It's one of the rules of the game.' My eyes fell from the shapes on the ceiling and down to those on the floor. 'Is it just me or are some of them getting closer?'

I glanced out through the shattered remains of one of the windows. The sun – already faint – was dipping behind a fat grey cloud. The barrier of light that kept the shadows off us was dimming fast.

'That's not good,' Ameena muttered. 'Do we have a plan?'

'Run?'

We looked towards the end of the corridor. It was tantalisingly close, but the wall of shadow still hung over it, blocking the way.

'Do we have another plan?'

I shook my head. 'The corridor round the corner is full of windows. Even with the sun blocked out there should be enough light coming in to stop them.'

Ameena scowled and stabbed a finger at the black blockade. 'And how are we going to get past that?'

'Like I said. *Run.*'

I charged forward as the last of the light faded at our feet. Behind us I heard a sickly, soggy *schlop*. The darkness was moving, no longer held back by the pale glow of the sun.

They were on me almost immediately, wrapping around my legs, tugging at my ankles. The light had weakened them, though, and I was moving too fast for them to get a proper grip.

Ameena moved even faster. She pulled level with me in a heartbeat, and I felt her hand grab on to mine as we approached the shimmering wall of shadow.

The darkness screeched. Angry shapes lashed out as we sprinted by, every step bringing us closer to the looming black barrier.

'Next time,' Ameena breathed, '*I* make the plan.'

And then suddenly we were leaping; throwing ourselves into the dark. It embraced us like quicksand, oozing around us, slowing us down. I stumbled on, pushing through the curtain of gunge, unable to see or hear Ameena, but still holding tightly to her hand.

I was running in slow motion. Every movement of every limb was difficult, as if gravity had been given a power-up.

Strands of silky black crawled across me, holding me back and dragging me down. Through it all I could feel Ameena's hand in mine. She powered ahead of me, dragging me through the inky gloop.

At last we tripped and fell out through the other side, landing in a heap on the floor next to another set of stairs. Pale light seeped in through an array of windows, burning up the few remaining slivers of darkness that clung to us.

The floor felt reassuringly solid beneath me as we sat there, taking a minute to get our breath back. Before us, the shadowy wall quivered and shook.

In a moment it had pulled back up into the ceiling. A second later, the shadowy shapes had begun retreating into the corners of the corridor. Another second after that and no one would have been able to tell they had ever been there in the first place.

'So,' Ameena began. 'You got another imaginary friend you didn't tell me about?'

I stood up, all too aware that time was running out for Billy. 'No. This one isn't mine.'

'So whose is it?'

'Billy Gibb's. The guy you saw me with earlier.'

'The kid who punched you? Should have guessed he'd have a big shadowy Hell-beast for a friend.'

'The shadows weren't his invisible friend,' I explained. 'She's a little girl with a doll.'

Ameena didn't even try to fight back her grin. 'That guy has a little girl with a dolly for an imaginary friend? That's priceless.'

'She's going to kill him if I don't find him.'

Her smile faltered a little, but didn't disappear. 'Serves him right.'

'I have to save him.'

Ameena hesitated for a millisecond. Then she nodded. 'Course you do, kiddo. That's what you superhero types always do.'

'I'm not a superhero.'

'Whatever you say,' she smirked. 'So, how do we find him?'

"There was an... wait. 'We'?"

'Yeah, well. Every hero needs a trusty sidekick.' Her grin spread further across her face. 'You can be mine.'

Despite the situation I smiled. I felt better having Ameena with me, and I hadn't asked her for help, so I hadn't broken any of Caddie's rules. Technically, at least.

'So how do we find him?' Ameena asked again.

'There were arrows,' I explained. 'I followed them here.'

'Were they absolutely massive and painted in blood?'

'Yes. Why, did you see them?'

'Nope.' She nodded towards the wall at the top of the next stairway. 'But I'm guessing they looked a lot like that one.'

Chapter Ten

CADDIE CADDIE HA-HA

We inched up the stairs, eyes rushing to examine every shadow we passed, in case it should move to attack us.

Ameena was a few steps above me, leading the way. I knew I should probably have been in front, but she'd barged past and – chicken as it was – I was relieved to let her go on ahead.

The third arrow was even bigger than the first two. As we approached it I realised the blood had not simply been smeared on this time. It was much creepier than that.

'OK. That's just disturbing,' Ameena whispered.

I could only nod in agreement, my eyes fixed on the wall. Hundreds of tiny, child-sized red handprints had been pressed against the white paint, forming the arrow's outline.

'Watch your feet,' warned Ameena, as she carried on up the stairs. I looked down and recoiled at the circular puddle of blood I was standing in. 'Floor's slippy.'

We carried on upwards, leaving wet crimson footprints on every step. For the first time since seeing the arrows I wondered whose blood had been used to make them. A shudder shook me by the shoulders. It must've taken gallons of the stuff to paint both those signs. How much blood did one human body hold?

And why had she painted the arrows anyway? She'd set me the challenge of finding Billy, and now she was leading me right to him? It didn't make any sense.

Unless, of course, she was leading me towards something else...

The top of the stairs came on us suddenly, and we stepped up into the mouth of a pale green corridor. It felt too open; too exposed. I had an urge to turn and run down the stairs, and I might have done, had Ameena not been with me. She took a faltering step forward and I followed close behind.

There were no arrows here, but we didn't need any to show us the way this time. One corridor led off in front of us, the other led off to the right. One was empty.

The other was not.

'You've got to be kidding,' Ameena snorted. 'We go from evil shadow puppets to this?'

I hesitated, sweeping my gaze slowly across the occupants of the corridor. 'It might not be what it looks like,' I whispered.

'No, I think it's *exactly* what it looks like,' she scoffed. 'And what it looks like is teddy bears with skipping ropes.'

It was hard to argue. Twelve dirty, torn teddy bears had

been attached to the wall and window frames – six on one side, six on the other. Between each one hung a grimy length of rope. Each rope dangled limply, forming a shape like the bottom half of a circle.

'OK,' I admitted. 'Maybe you're right.'

I studied the closest bear. It looked like road kill: filthy and threadbare, with only a few small patches of damp grey fur on its body. A tear that ran from the top of its head to halfway down its chest had been clumsily sewn together. Stuffing poked out through the stitches like fluffy internal organs. Two little dark holes in the fabric were all that remained of its eyes, the glassy eyes themselves presumably having been pulled out long ago.

Through its stomach, pinning the bear to the wall, was a large rusty nail. The nail also held the skipping rope in place.

The teddy was a freaky-looking soft toy, but a soft toy was all it was.

'This can't be it,' I muttered. 'There's got to be more to it than this.'

'Doesn't look like it to me,' Ameena answered. She shoved past me, reaching out for the bear. 'They're just a load of old—'

The teddy's head whipped round without warning. Its tiny jaws opened, briefly flashing two rows of pointed teeth, before the mouth snapped shut again just a few centimetres from Ameena's fingers.

We both froze, watching the bear writhe and twist as it fought to free itself from the nail in its belly. Its stubby arms were outstretched, flailing wildly at us, razor-sharp claws scratching at the air.

Ameena took a slow step back from the teddy, her eyes never leaving it. It hissed and snarled, struggling like a creature possessed. Strings of saliva hung from its jaws, flicking into the air with every movement of the bear's head.

The growling of the teddy seemed to waken the others. In a few seconds, all twelve bears were kicking their ragged legs, ripping at their chests with their short, stubby arms.

'So, this little girl,' Ameena whispered. 'Nutcase, is she?'

I nodded slowly. 'Oh yes.'

The bears thrashed around, growling and roaring. Realising it was trapped, the first teddy hurled back its head and unleashed a howl of torment and rage. The others followed suit, and soon the corridor rang out with their anguish.

I heard Ameena swallow hard. 'Can't wait to meet her.'

'That's lucky,' I breathed, looking past the bear now, to the end of the corridor where a white shape was standing, silent and still. 'You don't have to.'

Caddie watched us, unblinking. She lurked in the shadows, half concealed. I was just able to make out Raggy Maggie's porcelain head poking out of a pocket on the front of her dress. From here it almost looked like the doll was smiling.

The teddies on the wall seemed to sense her presence. They settled down into silence almost at once.

'That's her,' I whispered.

Ameena turned to me, her face impassive. 'I'd never have guessed.'

'Where's Billy?' I demanded. My voice echoed all the way along the corridor, but Caddie didn't answer. She simply held up her hands, and I realised she had a length of rope strung between them.

Without a word she arranged herself so the rope hung down at the back of her knees. Then, fixing me with her dead-eyed stare, she flicked the rope over her head and began to skip.

Tacka-tacka-tacka. The rope slapped off the floor every time she leapt over it. She sang along to the beat of her skipping, her high-pitched voice tuneless and flat.

'Caddie Caddie Ha-Ha,

Went to see her Papa,

Papa died, Caddie cried.

Caddie had a baby, named him Tiny Tim,

Put him in the bathtub to see if he could swim,

Drank down all the water,

Ate up all the soap,

Died the next morning with a bubble in his throat.'

She stopped skipping at that point, and I thought the rhyme was over. But she continued a moment later, this time in the harsh, scratchy tones of Raggy Maggie.

'Caddie called the doctor,

The doctor called the nurse,

The nurse called the lady with the alligator purse,

Mumps said the doctor,

Measles said the nurse...'

She took a sudden step towards us. The shadows fell away and I realised her white dress was stained all over with streaks of blood.

'*Dead* said the lady with the alligator purse.'

The way she spat out the word scared me.

'Who's dead?' I asked her. 'What do you mean?' She was retreating into the shadows now. 'Wait. Who's dead? It hasn't been an hour.'

'I told you no help,' she said, her voice her own now, lilting along the corridor. 'I told you all the rules.'

'Wait,' I cried, watching her slink back into the darkness until I couldn't see her any more. 'You said I couldn't *shout for help* – I didn't.' I hurried forward to stop her, but before I could take more than a few steps something flashed up before me and my hand exploded with pain.

I pulled back instantly. A flap of skin about the size of a pound coin was hanging off the back of my hand, just above the knuckle of my middle finger. Two thin rivers of blood trickled from each side of it, lazily zigzagging towards my wrist.

Along the corridor, six arcs of white were blurring through the air with an ominous *whum-whum-whum*.

The skipping ropes had started to move. And they were moving fast.

'You're going to want us to go through there, aren't you?' asked Ameena with a sigh.

'We need to get to Billy before it's too late.' On the wall, the hands of a clock ticked past the 2.45 mark. I had fourteen minutes left.

'I hate to say it, kiddo, but you heard her – it might already be too late.'

I didn't reply. I couldn't bring myself to believe that. If anything had happened to Billy then I was to blame. I might have wished him dead in the past, but I'd never meant it. Well, not really.

'There's another way,' I announced, remembering the other corridor. I started to backtrack towards it. 'We can go right round this floor and get past that way.'

'Now *that* sounds more like a plan,' Ameena replied. 'Much better than "run".'

It *was* a good plan. Or it would have been, at least.

I stopped at the entrance to the other corridor, unable to believe what I was seeing. Two minutes ago it had been clear, but now...

I stepped closer and let my fingers brush against the rough brickwork. It covered the entire opening to the English corridor. It felt solid. Real. But how?

'She built a wall,' I mumbled, hoping saying it out loud would somehow make it easier to accept. It didn't. I thumped my fist against the red stone in frustration. 'How could she build a wall?'

A low whistle escaped through Ameena's teeth. 'So... I guess we're skipping after all.'

I turned away from the barricade. The clock tocked over to 2.47. Another minute wasted. I was running out of time.

And so was Billy.

'Can you skip?' Ameena asked.

I watched the row of ropes whipping around and around through the air, too fast for my eyes to follow. 'Don't think so. You?'

'No idea. Never tried.'

'What? You've never tried skipping?' I frowned. 'But you're a girl.'

'I'm not even going to dignify that with a response.'

We took a few steps closer, until we could feel the wind from the first rope on our faces. The teddy bears were motionless, the ropes swinging freely from the nails in their guts.

Whum-whum-whum.

'Ready then?' Ameena sounded confident enough, but her eyes betrayed her.

'If we get hit...' I began, but I didn't need to finish. We'd both seen the cut on my hand. We both knew what would happen if we didn't manage to dodge the ropes.

Ameena bounced up and down on the balls of her feet. Her breath hissed rapidly in and out, as she psyched herself up.

'See you on the other side.'

She moved forward twice, hesitated both times, and then went on the third. I watched her duck her head and leap sideways into the blur. Her feet danced furiously on the lino for a moment, before she arched her back and jumped free of the first rope.

There was a thin film of sweat on her face, but she was smiling. *Smiling.*

'That was cool,' she grinned.

'Yeah, well, five more to go,' I reminded her, a little annoyed she'd made it look *quite* so easy.

'Hurry up then,' she urged.

'I'm coming,' I said. 'Give me a second.'

My eyes rolled like the reels of a fruit machine, trying to follow the blur of speed, looking for a gap; a way in.

'Tick, tock, tick, tock.'

'Shut up,' I hissed. 'I'm trying.'

'Well, try harder. Come on, it's easy.'

I ignored her, stepping back and focusing on the whirring of the rope. *Whum-whum-whum* it went, faster and faster and faster.

And then I saw it – the space I needed. I lurched forward in a heartbeat, making my move.

'*Wait!*' Ameena's voice was shrill and panicked. My legs heard it before the rest of me. They tried to stop, but my top half carried on regardless. I stumbled forward a few more steps, before finally managing to pull myself up just a centimetre from the rope.

'What? ' I gasped. 'What's wrong?'

'You were going to get your head cut off, that's what was wrong. You were miles off.'

'I wasn't,' I protested. 'I would have made it.'

'Want a tip?' she asked. 'Blink.'

'Blink?' I echoed. 'What are you on about?'

She fluttered her eyelashes. 'Blink,' she repeated. 'Quickly. Makes the rope easier to see.'

I didn't see how it could help, but I did as she suggested, opening and closing my eyes rapidly for a few seconds. Sure enough, the whirring rope slowed into a series of freeze-frames with every blink. It definitely made it easier to see the gap. Not easy, but eas*ier*.

'OK,' I muttered, rocking back and forth on the spot, 'here goes.'

I gulped down my nerves.

I blinked a little faster.

And then I jumped.

Chapter Eleven

CREAMING IT

I could hear screaming as I threw myself into the spinning tangle of rope, head down, arms pulled into my chest. The screams bounced around in the corridor, girly and annoyingly high-pitched.

It took me a few seconds to realise they were coming from me.

I was in the middle of the blur now, frantically jumping over and over as the length of cord *clacked* off the linoleum beneath me. My feet were dancing and my eyes were streaming and all around me was the *whum-whum-whum* of the rope.

Blinking didn't help. I was too close for the trick to work. Too close to freeze-frame the spinning streak of speed that guillotined the air above and below me.

My legs were tiring already. Any second now I'd misjudge a leap. Even the slightest mistake would cost me a foot, if not my life. I had to move.

Clack. I hopped over the rope and began to count.

Clack. A second. That was all I had. One sec—

Clack. I braced myself. This time.

Clack. I ducked sharply as I touched down on the floor, and fell, twisting my body to the right.

The edge of the rope brushed the back of my leg as I tumbled sideways, beyond its reach. I felt the ripple it made in the air even through my trousers.

'I did it!' I cried, springing upright next to Ameena. It was a huge relief, and I bounced up and down excitedly for a few moments, punching the air with joy.

'You did *one*,' she reminded me. 'Five left.'

My bouncing slowed to a gradual, slightly embarrassed stop. 'I know,' I said. 'It's just, you know? I did the first one.'

'Yay for you,' she said, clicking her tongue against the back of her teeth. 'Ready to go on?'

I glanced back at the clock and groaned. There were only ten minutes left until three o'clock. Ten minutes, five ropes and possibly another set of stairs to go. Even if Billy was right at the top of the steps, we'd be cutting it close.

'We're not going to make it,' I announced. 'There's not enough time.'

Ameena followed my gaze to the clock, then looked at the ropes spinning all along the length of the corridor. The next one was less than three metres away.

'Can't you do something?' she asked.

'Like what?'

'Blow them up or something, I don't know. Use your super—'

'Don't say it,' I snapped.

'We both know what you can do, Kyle,' Ameena said. The sentence stopped me in my tracks. I didn't remember her ever using my name before. It sounded strange coming out of her mouth. 'You turned a water pistol into a gun. You made *lightning*.'

'It was a thunderstorm,' I protested weakly. 'There was lightning anyway.'

'Not like that,' she replied, shaking her head. 'You made it happen. *You*.'

Stark images of Mr Mumbles leering at me from the darkness flashed before my eyes, and I felt my legs go weak. 'Can we not talk about that?' I murmured. 'I can't do anything. I told you, it's the rules.'

'Screw the rules!'

Whumwhumwhumwhum. The ropes seemed to be spinning faster. The six sounds combined to form a low whine that was steadily increasing in pitch, like a car engine accelerating. It made a knot of pain form just above my eyes.

'Caddie said something bad would happen if I used them.'

'Something worse than this?'

I hesitated. 'I... I don't know. Maybe. I don't want to use them unless there's no other choice. Only if it's, like, life or death.'

She thought for a moment, then gave a slight, barely noticeable nod of her head. 'Life or death, eh?' She glanced along the corridor to where the next rope was dicing the air. I saw her straighten up. I saw her fists clench.

I saw the next five seconds unfold before they'd even happened.

'No!' I cried, lunging, grabbing for her, my fingers finding only air. She was off and running, charging straight for the next rope. It accelerated further, as if somehow sensing her coming.

The *clacks* on the floor were just fractions of a second apart, and she was still running. The rope was going to slice her to ribbons *and she was still running*.

I couldn't have stopped the sparks flashing through my brain if I'd tried. They rushed upwards from the base of my skull, flooding my senses, more powerful than I'd ever felt them before.

I threw up a hand, focusing all my concentration on the closest rope, willing it to slow down. It whipped on, faster and faster. Ameena was almost on it. *Whip. Whip. Whip.* Another few steps and—

'STOP.' The word rolled from my mouth all by itself. I felt a surge of electricity crackle through me, and then the corridor was plunged suddenly into silence.

The ropes disintegrated into a soggy white mush. They sprayed outwards as they spun, showering the floor, ceiling and walls in thick blobs of goo.

Ameena skidded to a stop, sliding on the suddenly slippery floor. She turned, and I could see that she hadn't escaped the explosion of... *stuff,* either. Large dollops of it stuck to her face and hair. Without a word she scooped some off her cheek, sniffed it, then touched it with her tongue.

'It's cream,' she told me. 'Whipped cream.'

I dipped a finger into a blob on the wall and gave it an experimental taste. She was right. It was cream.

'This might sound ungrateful, what with you just saving my life,' she frowned. 'But *whipped cream*?'

'I... um... I don't know,' I shrugged, wiping the end of my finger clean on my jumper. 'I was trying to make the ropes stop, but...' I looked around at the mess. Even the teddy bears had been covered, although none of them were showing any reaction. '... I turned them to cream.'

She scooped a fat blob of white from her hair. 'That's just stupid.'

'Not as stupid as running at them head first,' I scolded. 'You could have been killed.'

'That was kind of the point,' she smirked. 'Life or death,

you said. I knew you wouldn't let me die.'

'And what if I couldn't do anything?' I demanded. 'Did you think of that?'

'No,' she admitted. 'Suppose I must have more faith in you than you do.' She glanced around at the streaks of white. They had begun to drip down from the ceiling and walls. 'Or I *did* have, anyway.'

I hurried past her along the corridor. 'Well, don't do anything like that again. I shouldn't be using this... this... whatever it is. I've broken the rules now. Something bad could happen.'

Ameena was at my heels, hurrying to catch up. I didn't look back, and instead kept my eyes locked on the stairs up ahead, trying to make it obvious how annoyed I was.

'But it hasn't, though,' she chirped. 'You used your magic mojo and nothing bad has happened.'

Something cut me off before I could reply.

Something bad.

A thunderous *boom* ripped through the school, shaking the building beneath us. The floor shuddered and lurched. I staggered, fighting to keep my balance, but a sudden onrushing wind smashed into me like an invisible battering ram, sending me sprawling backwards through the air.

With a grunt, I landed on my back between two of the teddy bears. They wailed and screeched, clawing furiously at the nails in their bellies, desperate to be free. From the way they moved I could tell it wasn't anger driving their frenzy, though.

It was fear.

Ameena was on the floor just in front of me. Her face was dirty and grey. She was screaming something, but my ears were still ringing from the blast and I couldn't make out a word.

And then she was on me, pushing me to the ground, shielding me. For a split second before she blocked my view I saw a billowing grey shape rushing up fast behind her.

Her hands felt warm on my face. She covered my eyes and blocked my mouth, protecting me from the cloud of choking grey dust that swept swiftly along the corridor.

When it found us, the swirling dust was hot and dry and rough as sandpaper. It lashed against me, stinging my skin as it howled over us, rushing to consume anything that stood in its way.

In a few seconds it had passed. Ameena lifted her hands away and I forced open my eyes. For a moment I thought an old woman was lying on top of me, until I realised it was the dust that had turned Ameena's hair grey.

'Um... thanks,' I said. My voice sounded faint and distant – drowned out by the tinny echo in my ears.

She nodded, but didn't speak. Her usual grin was gone from her face, and I could feel her whole body trembling.

We blinked wildly again as we stood up, this time in an attempt to keep the dust from our eyes. It hung in the air like a thick fog. It covered the floor and windowsills like dirty snow. Wherever I looked there was nothing but grey.

'Does that count as bad?' I coughed, swallowing the dryness at the back of my throat.

Ameena didn't seem to be listening. She was wringing her hands together, more frightened than I'd ever seen her before. 'She could have killed me,' she muttered, her voice a shocked whisper. 'That little psycho could have killed me.'

'Both of us,' I pointed out.

'What?' Ameena shook her head, as if clearing dust from her brain. I saw something flash across her face, as if she was remembering something she'd forgotten to do. 'Oh, yeah, that's what I meant.' She looked in the direction the cloud had come from, but the air was still too thick to see much. 'A bomb, you think?'

'I'm not... maybe,' was the only answer I could give. We made our way through the fog, still blinking away tiny particles of plaster and stone.

It was a good job the caretaker wasn't there to see the mess. He went mental if a window got broken, so there was no saying how he'd react to the English corridor being blown to bits. Probably not well.

'We need to move,' I said, painfully aware that Billy had virtually no time left. 'Can you see another arrow anywhere?'

'I can hardly see *you*.'

She had a point. The dust was so bad I was forced to feel my way along the wall. Lumps of stone and twisted fragments of metal were littering the floor. I kicked through the smaller chunks of debris, picked my way over the larger bits. All the while a steady *tick-tick-tick* in my head kept reminding me that if we didn't hurry, Billy would be putting the *dead* into *deadline*.

If he hadn't already.

My fingers brushed through a patch of wet on the wall. I took my hand away and found my fingertips stained with a thick red paste that crumbled and broke apart at my touch. It had a vaguely familiar coppery scent to it, as I held it to my nose and sniffed.

Ameena bumped into my back, jolting my hand into my face. The red sludge smeared across the bottom of my nose and on to my top lip. I tried spitting it out, but the dust had made my mouth dry.

'Sorry,' Ameena winced, realising what she'd done. 'What is that, anyway?'

Still spitting, I put my fingers back to the wall. The paste was smeared in a long, thin line. It went diagonally up at a forty-five degree angle. I couldn't reach the top, but I didn't have to. I knew what I'd find there. Two more lines sticking out from this one, forming the head of an arrow.

I looked at the wound on the back of my hand. The little red zigzags had turned into the same thick gunge.

'It's blood,' I said. 'It's blood mixed with dust.'

'Another arrow?'

'Pointing up,' I frowned. 'But I don't understand why it's here. The stairs don't start for another six or seven metres.'

I stepped away, wiping the crud off my face with the back of my sleeve. There was no time to worry about that now. We had to keep moving; had to reach Billy before it was too late.

I took a pace forward. Suddenly, a cool rush of air hit me from below. It fluttered up my trouser leg and I realised too late that there was no floor beneath me.

I had just stepped off into empty space.

Chapter Twelve

THE CLIMB

I yanked my leg back. My arms flailed and flapped like some demented bird, but it wasn't enough. I was falling.

The fog of dust was thinner down below, and as I toppled forward I could see all the way to the ground floor. How long would it take me to hit it? Three seconds? Five? Would I feel my bones break as I landed, or would I be dead before then? I'd find out soon enough.

Ameena casually caught me by the back of the jumper, steadying me. As the panic subsided, I realised I'd barely moved at all. I was standing at the edge of the drop, leaning over it only slightly. One step backwards and I'd have been safe. I took three steps, just to be sure.

'The stairs,' I gasped. 'She's demolished the stairs.'

'Looks like it,' Ameena nodded. She shook her head, almost smiling. 'Give her credit – for a five-year-old she's pretty resourceful.'

'She's also crazy,' I reminded her. 'And if we don't get to the next floor soon then Billy's going to find out just *how* crazy she is.'

The dust was slowly settling now, and I could see Ameena more clearly. She was coated from head to toe in the same powdery greyish-white as I was. Her dark eyes stood out, like two tiny lumps of coal on a snowman.

'Well then, we'd better get going,' she suggested.

'How? She blew up the stairs.'

'We climb.'

'Climb?' I gasped. 'What, up the walls?'

Ameena stepped closer to the edge. 'If you want,' she

shrugged. 'But I'll take the ladder.'

My eyes followed her as she reached into the fog and caught hold of a rope ladder that dangled down from somewhere out of sight above us.

'It's a trap,' I said suspiciously. 'It's got to be.'

'Course it is,' Ameena nodded. 'But unless you can magic us up a jetpack or something, I don't see any other way up.'

She stood there, one foot on the ladder, waiting for me to respond. When I didn't she began to climb.

'Come on,' she barked. 'It doesn't look far.'

Hesitantly, I took hold of one of the rungs. I tried to put my foot on to another, but the whole ladder swung away from me and I pulled back.

'I'm nearly there, come on,' Ameena called out. I craned my neck and peered through the settling dust. Sure enough, she was only eight or nine rungs away from the next floor.

I swung a leg out again, this time hooking it behind the

ladder so my heel rested on the rung. The rope didn't swing, and I managed to get my other foot up on to the next rung. I clung on, eyes fixed straight ahead, not daring to look down.

Somewhere above me was Caddie. Below me was a three-storey plummet to a messy death. I didn't know which one was worse.

Slowly, keeping my eyes locked dead ahead at all times, I lifted my lower foot from the ladder and moved it to the next rung. The ropes wobbled, and I held on so tight my knuckles turned white.

'Doesn't this seem weird?' I shouted, my voice shaking as badly as the ropes.

'Escaping flesh-eating teddy bears by climbing a rope ladder up to a five-year-old psychopath who doesn't really exist?' Ameena said. 'I don't know, is that weird, you think?'

'I mean...' I wasn't sure what I meant. Since escaping

the shadows, though, I'd had a nagging suspicion that Caddie somehow knew everything I was going to do. Like all this was part of her plan, and I was playing right into her hands. 'Forget it,' I said. 'You there yet?'

'Just about. Just a few more—' A panicked gasp cut her short. 'NO!' she screamed. 'No, don't! DON'T!'

I heard a childish giggle, and then in an instant I was falling. Dropping. Plunging towards the ground. The rungs of the ladder were still in my hands, but the ladder itself was plummeting with me.

I felt my heart speed up and my breath go short. She cut the ropes. *She cut the ropes.*

A buzz of electricity sliced across my scalp, but I was panicking too much to focus and it quickly slipped away. The ropes. *She cut the damn ropes.*

As I drew level with the first floor, the ladder suddenly went tight. The sharp stop made my feet slip from the rungs, sending my legs kicking frantically into thin air.

Something in my left shoulder went *pop* and exploded in pain. The arm went dead, and I could only watch as it slipped from the rung and dangled limply by my side, leaving me holding on with just one hand.

Above me I heard Ameena cry out in shock, and fight to hold on. Above *her* I heard that soft, high-pitched snigger again.

'You OK?' Ameena's voice was an urgent squeak. The dust was thin in the air, and I could see her without any problems. She was eleven or twelve rungs above me, hands and feet all still holding on. I'd managed to work my feet back into position, but my hand was sweating and becoming worryingly slippery.

'My shoulder,' I winced. 'I think I dislocated it.'

'Can you climb?'

I tried to lift my arm, but the pain was too much. I shook my head, defeated. 'No way.'

There was a pause, and then the ladder began to shake

gently, as Ameena climbed back down.

Just before she reached me, she curled a leg round and switched to the opposite side of the ladder. I was amazed at how easily she could move around on the rungs. It was like she'd done this a thousand times before.

She clambered down a few more steps until our feet shared the same rung. With all the weight now near the bottom, the ladder began swinging back and forth like an enormous, slow-moving pendulum.

'I need you to hold on to me,' she instructed.

I hesitated, and felt my cheeks go red. Luckily the thick layer of grime on my face covered up my embarrassment. 'Um... what?'

She put one arm round me and grabbed me by the back of the jumper, pulling me in against the ladder. 'Like that,' she said. 'Tight.'

Her grip held me up as I cautiously let go of the ladder. When I was sure I wasn't about to fall, I reached round behind her and caught hold of the back of her jacket. There wasn't a lot of material to grab on to, but I found a strap and buckle and wrapped my fingers around that.

'You got me?' she asked. When I nodded she said, 'Good.'

My arm took her weight as she let go of me. For one terrifying moment I thought I would fall, until I realised her weight was holding me up, just as I was holding her.

The tip of her tongue poked out in concentration as she rested her left hand on my left shoulder. Her right hand took hold of my upper arm. She held it firmly, and I had to bite my own tongue to stop myself whimpering in pain.

She peered at me through the curtain of her straggly hair. Her mouth was smiling, but her eyes were not.

'Whatever you do,' she said, 'don't let go.'

'I won't,' I promised. 'Why would I let go?'

The pain stole my words away. It tore through my shoulder and across my back. A howl burst from my lips and tears sprang to my eyes. The fire burned along my arm and the world whirled and spun until my head went light. I was going to be sick.

'*Don't let go!*' The urgency in Ameena's voice cut through the pain. I hadn't noticed my grip slipping on her back, but I tightened it just in time to stop us falling in opposite directions.

I tried to speak, but the words came out as a blubbering mess of sobs. 'What... what... did you do?'

'Shoulder's not dislocated any more,' she said, so matter-of-factly I almost wanted to punch her. She took her hands away from me and caught hold of the ladder again. 'How does it feel?'

'How do you think it feels?' I snapped. 'Bloody sore.'

Her whole face grinned at me. 'Yeah, but not *as* sore, I bet.'

I moved the arm around slowly, testing it out. The initial burst of pain had faded, and I was now left with just a dull, throbbing ache. 'It still hurts,' I grunted, not wanting to admit she was right.

'So *now* can you climb?'

I looked up. I could see the top of the ladder, but it was a long way away.

'Ladies first,' I nodded.

'OK,' Ameena said, still smiling. 'Off you go then.'

'Hilarious,' I sneered. Arm aching, I reached to the next rung and began to climb up the shaky rope ladder.

Having Ameena beneath me made climbing easier. Her weight stopped the ladder swinging, and despite my sore shoulder we were halfway to the top in no time.

At every step I expected the ladder to fall again, but even by the three-quarter point it hadn't moved. Despite that, I couldn't work up the nerve to look down at the floor, so dizzyingly far away.

'You know what I don't understand?' Ameena didn't even sound out of breath.

'What?'

'Why change the theme?'

I let the sentence roll around inside my head for a few moments, to see if it would start to make some kind of sense. It didn't.

'Change what theme?'

'Well, think about it,' she said. 'We had evil shadow puppets, right?'

'Don't remind me.' Both my arms were aching now, but I pushed on. Fourteen rungs to go.

'OK. So then it was teddy bears and skipping ropes.'

'And an explosion,' I added.

'Forget the explosion for now,' she said.

'It's not an easy thing to forget.' Thirteen rungs.

'Shut up and listen. Shadow puppets. Teddy bears. Skipping ropes. It's all kiddie stuff. It's all for little kids.'

'She *is* a little kid,' I pointed out.

'Exactly.'

I dragged myself up another rung. Twelve left. It was taking all my strength to hang on. I didn't have the energy for this conversation.

'What's your point?' I asked.

'So why a ladder? Why not a trampoline or... like... a giant catapult or something?'

'Because that would be stupid.' Eleven.

'OK, fine, but why blow up the stairs if it didn't fit in with the other stuff?'

'Not sure,' I spat. 'Maybe because she's a psycho?'

'No doubt,' Ameena agreed. 'But she's a psycho with a *theme*. Toys and games. There's no such game as *Ladder*.'

My hand found the next hold. Ten to go.

'Not that I know of,' I admitted. 'But so what?'

'I dunno,' Ameena sighed. 'Maybe it's nothing. Maybe I'm wrong. It's just... *Oh my God!*'

'What?' I cried, startled by her panicked tone. 'What is it?'

'It's a snake. A giant snake. Move, move, *move!*'

A sharp *hiss* rose up from somewhere below me. *Snakes and ladders.* Of course. I should have guessed.

Terror lent my limbs an unexpected burst of energy, and I virtually leapt the next few rungs.

'It's coming,' Ameena wailed. 'Faster, move faster.'

Four rungs left. Another hiss. Something brushed against the back of my leg, and I let out an involuntary cry of fright.

'Move, Kyle, it's right behind you!'

Muscles burning, I caught hold of the broken edge of the third floor and flung myself up. I rolled clumsily, and jumped upright, eyes fixed on the spot where the floor fell away, ready to face whatever rose above it.

It was Ameena's head that appeared. Tears cut through the grey dust on her cheeks. She was shaking as she pulled herself up.

Shaking with laughter.

'Man, you fall for that every time,' she gasped, lying on

her back on the floor, barely able to get breath through her giggles. 'You should see your face.'

'You idiot! I nearly had a heart attack,' I snapped, but that only made her worse.

It wasn't until a few seconds later, when she stood up, that she stopped laughing. She stared past me, eyes wide, pretending to be shocked by something at my back.

'Behind you. Turn round,' she said. Her voice was a stark whisper. It was an Oscar-worthy performance, but I wasn't buying it.

'I'm not falling for that again,' I said, crossing my arms across my chest.

She swallowed. 'I'm not kidding this time. Promise.'

'You're not fooling me again,' I sniffed. '*But* I'm going to turn round anyway, because we need to go. We're almost out of time. That's why I'm turning round, not because of your stupid trick.' Feeling pleased with myself, I turned away from her.

Caddie stood blocking the entrance to the corridor. Her hands were on her hips and her bottom lip stuck out.

'You're late,' she sulked, stamping her foot down. The flat heel of her shoe barely made a sound against the dusty floor.

The doll was still in her dress pocket. Still staring at me. For a moment I could have sworn a smile played at the corners of its painted mouth. 'And people who are late,' seethed Caddie, 'make Raggy Maggie *very* cross indeed.'

Chapter Thirteen

THE RED ROOM

"Where's Billy?' I demanded. 'What have you done with him?'

'One hour, that's what I said,' Caddie scowled. 'You took one hour and five more minutes. That's not even close.'

'Where is he?' I repeated, more firmly this time. 'And everyone else – what did you do with everyone else?'

'Not telling. You didn't win the game.'

I leapt for her, suddenly furious. My fingers tightened around the top of her arms. Her shoulders felt skinny and weak in my grip. 'It's not a game,' I snarled. 'None of this is a game. Now tell me where they are.'

Something cold and sharp exploded inside my head, as if an ice pick had been stabbed into my brain. My legs buckled and I crumpled to my knees. As my hands fell away from Caddie's arms the pain quickly began to ease.

'That's for not playing nicely,' she whispered.

'B-Billy,' I wheezed, 'where... where is he?'

'Tell him.' Ameena couldn't hide the contempt in her voice. 'Now.'

Caddie gave a giggle and pirouetted away, twirling a strand of her hair around a pale finger. 'Don't remember,' she said. 'I put him *somewhere*, but...'

The sentence drifted off, as if she'd forgotten how it was supposed to end. Her delicate features pulled into a frown. Slowly, she reached into her dress pocket and pulled out the doll.

'What's that you say, Raggy Maggie?' she asked. Ameena helped me up as Caddie held the doll's porcelain head next to her own ear. 'But I don't want to tell him. He wasn't nice to me. He didn't win the game.'

Raggy Maggie's head moved up and down sharply in Caddie's hand. For a long time the girl just stood there, her expression becoming darker and darker, as she "listened" to what her dolly had to say.

'It's not fair,' Caddie spat at last. She shoved Raggy Maggie back into her pocket and jabbed a finger in the direction of a pale orange door. 'He's in *there*, OK?'

I glanced from the door to Caddie and back again. The door led into a stationery cupboard, I knew. I'd been sent to collect pencils and things from there before. It was long and wide, with shelves lining every side. There were no windows inside it, and no other way in or out.

Another trap? Maybe. Probably. But there was only one way to know for sure.

I approached the door, listening for any sign of life inside. I heard nothing. Caddie's eyes were on me when I looked back over my shoulder. They sparkled with something between mischief and malice.

'Watch her,' I told Ameena, and I turned to the door again.

The metal handle pushed down with a *click*. Cautiously, I inched the door open a crack. As I did, a warm wetness seeped from within and washed over my shoes.

I heard Caddie giggle as a river of red rushed out from inside the cupboard. It pooled around my feet, settling into a thick and gloopy puddle.

Sour saliva formed at the back of my throat. I had to swallow it down to stop myself being sick.

The door gave a creak as I pushed it open the rest of the way. Dim daylight cut through the darkness of the windowless room and I felt my heart skip several beats.

For a moment I thought the room was bleeding. The shelves and the walls glistened under a covering of crimson. The blood dripped from the ceiling, from the light shade, from the pens and the pencils and the spiral-bound notebooks.

And it dripped from Billy.

He was sitting on a chair at the very back of the cupboard. Head down. Not moving. His hands were behind the chair's back, tied the same way I had been.

Drip. Drip. Drip. The sound was on all sides of me as I stepped into the little room, like the plinks and plonks of a broken xylophone.

'Billy,' I said, my voice a shrill whisper. 'Billy, are you OK?'

It was a stupid question. He was tied to a chair and drenched in blood. Of course he wasn't OK.

I crept forward, until I was just a few paces away. Billy still wasn't moving. His head hung at a worrying angle. Droplets of blood dangled from the end of his nose like tiny red icicles. I watched one of them wobble, then fall. It made a tiny splash where it landed in the puddle on the floor.

My hand was trembling as I held it out, palm down. I should shake him on the shoulder. I was *going* to shake him on the shoulder, but fear tightened my muscles and made it hard to move. What if he didn't respond? What if he didn't wake up?

What if she'd killed—

A startled cry escaped my throat as Billy's head suddenly lifted, revealing a face that was a mass of black and blue bruises. One sharp gasp of breath filled his lungs, and his eyes flicked open. The pupils swam lazily, as if he wasn't quite conscious.

'You're alive,' I cried. 'Thank God.'

His head rolled loosely on his shoulders. He tried to speak, but the words came out as spittle on his swollen lips.

'Of course he's alive, silly.'

I spun to find Caddie standing just outside the stationery cupboard, still clutching her doll. I couldn't see Ameena anywhere.

'Where's Ameena? What have you done with her?'

'Your daddy told us you'd be fun to play with,' Caddie

giggled, ignoring the question. 'And he was right. This has been lots of fun, hasn't it?'

'And killing Billy?' I scowled. 'Would that have been fun too?'

'I would never hurt Billy,' Caddie protested. 'Billy's my bestest friend in the whole wide world.' She glanced down at Raggy Maggie. 'Well... second bestest.'

I heard a low groan tumble from Billy's mouth. 'But you did hurt him,' I said. 'Look at him. He's a mess.'

Caddie shook her head. 'That wasn't me. That was Raggy Maggie.' She patted the doll's head. 'Raggy Maggie was very cross with Billy, but I told her it wasn't his fault. It wasn't his fault he forgot about us.'

Her face twisted into a mask of rage. 'It was *her* fault.'

I blinked. 'Who? The doll?'

'No. Not Raggy Maggie. *Her!*' Caddie's tiny hands were clenched into fists. '*She* had to come along and spoil everything. It's *her* fault we had to go away to the dark place.'

'Billy?' I frowned. 'What's she talking about?'

Billy's eyes were more focused now, but his whole body was trembling. He shook his head from side to side, sending droplets of blood spraying across the room. 'I couldn't help it,' he spluttered. 'She m-made me tell her. I'm sorry.'

'What?' The panic in Billy's eyes set alarm bells ringing in my head. 'What do you mean?' I asked him. 'Sorry for what?'

'We would *never* have killed Billy,' Caddie said. 'We didn't even hurt him *that* badly.'

'But... the blood. Here on the walls. And the arrows...'

'That's not Billy's blood.'

A strangled sob caught in the throat of the boy behind me. 'I'm sorry,' he wept. 'She made me tell her. *She made me.*'

'Whose blood is it?' I asked. There was a tone to my voice I'd never heard before, as if someone else was speaking for me. My pulse had suddenly started racing. Every breath I took was becoming more difficult, as my chest went tight.

'It wasn't fair her coming along like that,' Caddie sniffed. 'She made all the bad things happen. She made Billy forget all about us.'

My lips had gone dry, but the rest of me felt soaked with sweat. 'Whose blood is it?' I said again.

'Our game was just meant to keep you busy.' Caddie clapped her hands excitedly. 'So me and Raggy Maggie could play a game that was much more fun.'

'My sister,' Billy sobbed. 'She's got my little sister.'

For a moment everything in the world seemed to stop. Everything, that is, but the *drip, drip, drip* of the droplets of red.

'Lilly?' I croaked. 'It's Lilly's blood?'

'Oh no, it's not *hers*,' Caddie giggled. 'I haven't done anything to her yet.'

'Then whose is it?'

Caddie's voice came as a thin and scratchy whisper. 'It's your mummy's.'

A numbness froze me, made it impossible to move. The words rattled around in my head, empty and meaningless, as if my mind was rejecting them, pushing them away.

Behind me, Billy was babbling. Weeping. Wailing. *I'm sorry. I'm sorry. I'm sorry.*

'That's what she gets for looking after *her*—'

'You're lying,' I said.

'Only bad girls tell lies.'

'You're lying!' I hurled myself at her. It wasn't true. It couldn't be true. I'd make her confess. Make her admit it was all just another of her sick little jokes.

That icy blade cut through the inside of my head again, cold and sharp, slicing through my every thought. I didn't feel my legs go limp. Didn't feel my jaw crack off the blood-drenched floor. Didn't feel *anything* but the freezing fire burning through my brain.

It was a struggle, but I managed to crane my neck enough to find Caddie. She was hazy and indistinct, but I could see she was still standing outside the door. One hand was resting on the handle. In the other hand she clutched Raggy Maggie. The doll's single eye leered down at me, merciless and unblinking. Where was Ameena when I needed her?

'You know, maybe I *am* lying,' Caddie sang. Her voice echoed, like feedback at a concert. 'Maybe I'm not. But it doesn't really matter.'

I heard the door creak, saw the light narrowing and the shadows growing. I fought with my legs, but they weren't working. I could do nothing but lie there and watch as Caddie's face distorted into an inhuman grin that was much too wide for her face.

'It doesn't matter, because you'll never know,' she whispered.

The door closed over with a slam, leaving me all alone

in the cupboard with Billy and the swirling, flowing rivers of blood.

Chapter Fourteen

COMPLETE SURRENDER

With the door closed the air in the room was choking. It smelled like the contents of a butcher's bin bag. It stunk of rancid things. Rotting things. Things days dead. It swirled up my nostrils and nipped at my lungs as I hauled myself up and shook the fuzz from inside my head.

Billy was babbling and whimpering. Noises, not words. Normally it would have been distracting. Normally it would have shot my concentration to pieces.

Normally.

But not now.

Now the sparks raced and danced and crackled – not

just across my head this time, but through my every vein. I could feel them there, just below my skin, pushed around my body by a swelling of hatred and rage. I couldn't have stopped them, even if I'd wanted to.

And I didn't want to. I was no longer holding back. I'd felt their power on Christmas Day. I'd sensed then what the sparks could do – what *I* could do – and I'd been afraid. Afraid to give in to it. Afraid to test the extent of my new abilities.

I wasn't afraid any more.

It's your mummy's. Caddie's voice played over and over in my head, scratchy and crackling, like an old vinyl record.

She hurt my mum.

The hairs on my arms and the back of my neck stood up. Static electricity fizzled on my skin.

She hurt my mum.

Something in my vision flickered, and the dark was

pushed aside by a ghostly blue glow. It picked out the edges of everything. The shelves. The door. Billy, mouth open, weeping silently.

She hurt my mum.

And she was going to pay.

My finger lifted, touched the door. The wood exploded into matchsticks, letting the light flood in.

I stepped out of the cupboard. Caddie was already gone, and it looked like she had taken Ameena with her. I wasn't sure how she could have done it, but there was a lot more to the little girl than her appearance suggested.

I didn't know where she had gone to. Right then, I didn't care. I knew where I was going, and that was enough. Behind me Billy swallowed down a sob.

'How... how did you d-do that?'

'Long story,' I said. 'Caddie. How fast can she move from place to place?'

'W-what?'

'When she was in your head,' I said. 'Back then, how quickly did she move?'

'I don't know,' Billy replied. 'I never really saw... usually if I went anywhere she'd get there ahead of me. She'd just kind of be there waiting for me.'

'Great,' I sighed. That was just what I didn't want to hear. I started to stride towards the hole where the stairs should have been. 'You coming?' I asked, not looking back.

'I can't,' he croaked. 'My hands. I'm tied.'

'No,' I said, picturing the ropes falling away. 'You aren't.'

The chair creaked as he got up. 'How did you—?'

'I don't have time to explain,' I snapped. 'Now move.'

His feet splashed through the blood – through my mum's blood – as he scurried out of the store cupboard. The shattered edge of the floor was a few paces in front of me. I broke into a run. As I did, I heard Billy's feet hesitate and a gasp stick in his throat.

'Watch out!' he warned. 'You're going to fall.'

I saw the stairs as they should have been, and my insides sparkled like a sack of diamonds. I didn't bother to look down as I stepped off the edge. Didn't bother because I knew I had nothing to fear.

The first step appeared as my foot came down, the empty air turning to solid stone just in time to support me. A second step formed next to it, lower down. By the time I'd reached the third step, the entire stairway had been rebuilt.

Billy cautiously lowered a foot on to the top step and touched it with the toe of his shoe. When it didn't move, he ventured down a couple more steps.

'That's... impossible,' Billy whispered. 'It's impossible,' he repeated, louder this time. His footsteps broke into a gallop, and within a few seconds he was running beside me down the stairs. 'How did... I mean...?'

'What did you tell her?' I asked him.

'What? I don't—'

'What did you tell her?'

We passed the second floor and carried on down the steps. The light from the window reflected off the dampness in Billy's eyes.

'She... she asked about my sister,' Billy began. 'About Lilly. She knew all about her. She wanted... She asked me where she was.'

'And you told her?' I sneered. 'Just like that.'

'No, not just like that.' Billy's voice took on a little of its usual edge. Not much, but a little. 'I told her to get out of my face. Told her I wasn't telling her nothing.'

'But you did tell her.' I didn't make any attempt to hide the anger in my voice. 'Didn't you?'

Billy's mouth flapped up and down for a few seconds, like a fish stuck on dry land. The first floor passed. We were almost at the bottom.

'She... did things,' Billy said. He sounded hollow and mechanical. From the corner of my eye I saw him lift up his school jumper and the shirt beneath it.

The skin on his chest and stomach was scalded red. Here and there it formed into bulbous blisters. A clear liquid sloshed about inside them as we hurried down the last of the steps.

'I tried not to tell her,' he said hoarsely, 'but she wouldn't stop.' His hands were shaking as he pulled the clothes back down. I glanced up into eyes I no longer recognised. Tears rolled down Billy's cheeks, cutting tracks through the drying blood. 'I tried,' he sobbed, 'but she wouldn't stop. *She wouldn't stop so I told her where Lilly was. I told her she was at your house.*'

His whole body was shaking now. I should have hated him. I *wanted* to hate him. He'd not only sold out his own little sister, he'd sold out my mum. But I remembered the pain that had spilled from Caddie's teapot. Billy had given in to it. Who was to say I wouldn't eventually have done the same?

Mum would have tried to protect Lilly. She'd have done everything she could to keep the girl safe.

She wouldn't have stood a chance.

'What then?' I asked.

'She... she left. She locked me in. I didn't see her again until you arrived.'

We were down the stairs now, running towards a side door of the school. Beyond that lay the staff car park. Beyond that a three-mile journey home. I wasn't sure if Caddie would be there, but Mum might be, and right then, that was all I cared about.

'How long was she gone?'

'I... I don't know.'

The anger inside me lashed out. 'Well, *think*, Billy.'

'I was... I passed out,' he protested weakly. 'I don't know, I'm sorry.'

The doors flew open before we'd reached them and we exploded out into the car park. There were around two dozen cars parked in it. Wherever the staff and pupils of the school had gone, they hadn't driven there.

An hour and five minutes – that was how long it had taken me to get to Billy. I'd seen Caddie about ten minutes before I made it to the top floor, so that was a fifty-five minute period when I didn't know where she was or what she was doing.

Fifty-five minutes. Was that enough time to torture Billy, get to my house, then get back? It depended on how long Billy took to crack. It was a twenty-minute round trip by car from my house to school. I doubted Caddie could drive, but the girl was full of surprises.

So thirty-five minutes to get what she needed from Billy, attack my mum and snatch Lilly. Much as I hated to admit it, it was doable. It was definitely doable.

'Where are we going?' Billy asked.

'My house.' I eyed up the cars, trying to find one that looked fast. I quickly realised none of them did. Most of the teachers drove boring, sensible vehicles that would struggle to hit fifty miles per hour. *Most* of the teachers.

But not all of them.

Mr Preston was very protective of his motorbike. It was black, red and silver. It was also ridiculously shiny. It stood there glistening and sleek in the sunlight. Mr Preston's pride and joy.

A spark flashed through me and the bike roared into life.

'Whoa,' Billy whistled. 'How did you do that?'

'Will you stop asking me that?' I spat.

Billy fell silent. He watched me swing my leg over the bike. It hummed impatiently beneath me. 'Do you know how to ride?' he asked meekly.

'I'll learn. Get on.'

He hesitated for a second, then clambered on behind

me. I was trying to figure out how to make the bike start moving when I realised someone was standing in front of me. It was the man who had untied me from the chair in the canteen.

'Do me a favour,' he said, holding up both hands. A motorbike helmet was perched on each palm. 'If you're going to head off on this contraption, at least stick these on. Last thing you need is your head bashed in.'

He passed me one of the helmets. It was black with a clear visor, and I recognised it as Mr Preston's. It tugged at my ears as I slipped it over my head, and everything suddenly sounded distant and muted.

I had a lot of questions I would have liked to ask the mystery man, but once again there was no time. I settled on only one.

'How's Mrs Milton?'

'She's fine,' he said, handing the other helmet to Billy. 'Bit confused, but fine. She doesn't remember any of it.'

'Lucky her,' I muttered.

'Hey! Not fair,' Billy complained. He was holding the other helmet up, scowling at it as if it were covered in sick. 'How come I get the pink one?'

'Just put it on,' I told him.

'Good luck,' the man said. He stepped aside, making room for us to pass.

'Oh, come on, it's got *Sexy Mama* written on it!'

'Will I see you again?' I asked, ignoring Billy's protests.

'I mean... *Sexy Mama*!'

The man nodded. 'I hope so.'

Billy said something else, but he was halfway through putting the helmet on, and his voice was muffled. I kicked the motorbike stand away and twisted the throttle. The bike suddenly launched us forward and Billy's words were left trailing in our wake. Whatever he had said, it wasn't important. Nothing was important. Nothing mattered but getting home.

The white lines and tarmac flew by beneath us, and we were out of the car park in seconds. I wrenched on the handlebars and took the corner awkwardly. The bike weaved wildly on to a narrow side road, the engine shuddering and stuttering as we left the school behind.

I twisted the right handle, opening the throttle further. The back wheel spun and the engine squealed in complaint, but the burst of speed helped keep the bike balanced. Tyres smoking, we screeched off towards the main road.

Billy's voice came crackling from somewhere by my right ear. The helmets must have some kind of communication system built in, I realised. 'We are *so* going to die,' Billy groaned.

I didn't answer. The motorbike had seemed like a good idea. I'd pictured it kicking into life, and it had done just that. Picturing myself as someone who could actually ride a motorbike, though – that was proving more difficult.

The main road was a hundred metres ahead. One left turn and three miles and we'd be within spitting distance of my house. It sounded simple. I gritted my teeth and thought of Mum. It *would be* simple.

Traffic flowed in both directions along the main road. The town wasn't big enough to have a proper rush hour – and even if it did this wouldn't have been it – but there was still a stream of cars racing past the T-junction ahead of us.

Sure, I thought. *Simple.*

We wobbled our way up to the junction. I had slowed down, but didn't want to stop. I wasn't sure if I could keep the bike balanced if we stopped. Besides, stopping would waste time.

A white van flashed past, probably over the speed limit. A silver car shot by behind it. The driver's eyes went wide as he spotted us – two kids riding a motorbike – but he didn't slow down.

There was a break in the traffic after that, although I

could see a white car coming up fast. The rage had made me confident – more confident than I'd ever felt – but now that confidence was fading a little. The white car was closing the gap. This was going to be tight.

'Hold on,' I yelled, twisting the grip and accelerating out on to the main road.

'Hey, cool, we can hear each other,' Billy said, but I was too focused on what I was doing to reply.

The bike lurched, stuttered a few times, then began to speed up. I glanced down at the digital speedometer in the centre of the handlebars. It said we were going at twenty-seven miles per hour, but that couldn't be right. It felt much faster.

'Change gears,' instructed Billy. 'You're going to blow the engine up.'

Up until that point I hadn't realised motorbikes had gears. Now he mentioned it, though, the whine of the engine was getting higher and higher, like a swarm of angry wasps.

'How do I do that?' I asked.

An arm appeared over my left shoulder. The finger was extended towards the left handle grip.

'Twist that, then there's a little lever next to your right foot,' he instructed. 'Click that.'

It took a few tries, but I eventually managed a clumsy gear change. The bike roared furiously for a few moments, then settled down into something resembling a normal engine sound.

'Keep changing up as we get faster,' Billy told me. I nodded and clicked the bike into third gear, then fourth. The transitions got smoother each time, and the bike didn't complain nearly as much. I glanced at the speedo again. Fifty-four miles per hour. That was more like it.

'How did you know about the gears?' I asked, bending my body forward against the wind.

'My cousin has a bike,' he explained. 'He's let me ride it a few times.'

'And you didn't think to mention that *before* we got on?' I scowled.

'I thought you knew what you were doing.'

'Well, I don't.'

I had to breathe deeply to stop my anger bubbling over. My whole body still felt alive with electricity. I was a loaded weapon, ready to go off. If I didn't calm down there was no saying what could happen.

We were on our way, that was the main thing. All we had to do was follow the main road for another couple of miles. Just five minutes or so and I'd be home.

A white shape appeared in one of the bike's wing mirrors. I flicked my eyes from the road long enough to make out the white car. It was directly behind us, dangerously close.

In the front seats, two men stared, slack-jawed with shock. On the roof above them, a set of blue lights screamed into action.

'It's the police,' Billy yelped.

'I know,' I spat. For a moment I thought about stopping. For a moment I thought about pulling over and telling them everything.

But only for a moment.

I opened the throttle all the way and the numbers on the speedometer began to climb.

'What... what are you doing?' wailed Billy.

The sparks inside me fizzled and danced. 'Relax,' I smirked. 'It's a getaway.'

Chapter Fifteen

THE CHASE

The sirens of the police car became fainter as the bike pulled away. The wind whipped at me, pressing against me like a hand against my chest. The tail lights of the silver car in front grew steadily larger – two glowing red eyes in the faint January daylight, rushing up to meet us.

'Slow down,' Billy cried.

I didn't. Instead I shifted my weight and nudged the handlebars. The bike edged sideways and we shot past the silver car, close enough to touch it. The driver's eyes were still wide and staring as we roared by him. Behind us the police siren screeched louder as they also hurried to overtake the other car.

This was madness. I'd never even sat on a motorbike before today, and now I was riding one in a high-speed police chase. What was I thinking?

Billy's voice crackled in my ear. 'We'll go to jail for this.'

'Maybe not,' I replied. 'We might die first.'

There was a pause, before Billy spoke again. 'That doesn't make me feel better.'

'How are we doing?' I asked. Even through the helmet intercom I was having to raise my voice to make it heard above the roaring of the engine and the wailing of the siren.

I felt Billy twist in his seat. When he turned back he said, 'Not great.'

'How close?'

'About eight or nine metres.'

The power inside me throbbed. It ran like a shiver along

the length of my spine and sat there at the base of my skull. Lurking. Waiting for me to set it free.

I could crush the police car. I could yank it off course, send it smashing into a wall. I could blow it to pieces with just a thought. I could do *anything*, and there would be no way for them to stop me.

The electricity buzzed impatiently in my head, rattling my teeth in their sockets. The wheels of the bike swallowed up the road. We were less than a mile from my house now. I had to get rid of the police. They couldn't be allowed to slow me down, even if that meant killing them.

No! I shook my head, pushing away all thoughts of killing anyone. The power within me hissed and spat, like a wild animal trapped inside a cage. What was happening to me?

'More bad news.' Billy's voice startled me. The handlebars wobbled in my grip, sending the bike weaving on to the wrong side of the road. A horn blared. I hauled the bike left, just in time to avoid a head-on collision with another car.

'What is it?'

Billy pointed towards the wing mirror. I glanced in it. The road behind was filled with blue lights now, all flashing together.

'Another car and two motorbikes,' Billy shouted. 'It's no use, we need to stop.'

'My mum might be dead,' I roared. 'Your little sister might be dead. Do you really want me to stop?'

Billy's tone was uncertain. 'Maybe they can help.'

'They can't help, Billy. No one can help us.'

'But they'll catch us. We can't get away.'

'We can,' I argued. I focused on one of the sparks that flashed around inside me. Could I do this? Could I go there again? And if I could, could I take someone else along with me? I had to try.

'How?' Billy demanded.

The spark I concentrated on slowed down almost immediately – much quicker than had happened before. My mind shut around it like a steel trap, pinning it in place.

'Because I know a shortcut,' I announced, as the world around us began to shimmer and change. 'Now hold on tight and close your eyes. And whatever you do, don't open them again until I say so.'

The surface of the road was a spider's web of cracks. Weeds and moss grew and twisted through the gaps, pushing the chunks of broken stone further apart. The bike's wheels bounced hard on the uneven ground, throwing us around on the seat.

The sirens had stopped. The police cars were no longer in sight. There wasn't a whole lot in sight, for that matter. A dark, desolate landscape stretched out in all directions. Here and there the ruined remains of buildings jutted out of the ground, like broken, rotting teeth from a diseased gum.

A mile or so ahead lay a warped mirror image of my village. Even from this distance I could hear the howls and screams of the creatures that inhabited it.

'Whoa!' Billy cried. 'Where are we? How did you do that? Why is it so dark?'

'I told you to keep your eyes closed.'

I'd done it. I'd actually brought Billy with me. I could barely believe it. Now all I had to do was keep us alive long enough to get back out.

'Is this Hell?' asked Billy, his voice tinged with panic. 'It's Hell, isn't it? We crashed, and now we're in Hell. Well that's just great...'

'It's not Hell,' I said. 'Well, not the one you're thinking of, anyway. You know how Caddie went away when you stopped thinking about her?'

Billy sounded embarrassed talking about it. 'Yeah.'

'This is where she went. I think... I think this is where they all go. Imaginary friends. When they're forgotten.'

He pushed air out through his teeth as he looked around. 'Wow,' he muttered. 'No wonder she went nuts. Is this where yours went?'

'Yep.'

'And was he crazy?'

I felt Mr Mumbles' hands at my throat again. Saw his stitched-up lips. Smelled his rotten-meat stench. 'Pretty much,' I said.

I pulled the bike off the road and on to the hard-packed desert floor that lined either side. It was smoother than the shattered tarmac, and the bike's vibrations eased away a little as the tyres found traction.

Twisting the throttle, I sent the motorcycle roaring across the dusty ground, front wheel aiming for the village. I didn't dare go as fast here – the scorched ground was much more uneven than the road we'd left behind – but at least there was no danger of a police roadblock springing up in front of us.

The howling and screeching and wailing of the creatures in the village rose in volume as we drew closer. I felt Billy shudder in the seat behind me, but was surprised to find my own hands were rock steady. It was a stillness born of determination – I knew what I had to do, and I would let nothing stop me.

As we reached the first of the village's buildings I slowed the bike to a stop. A few shadowy figures scurried across the far end of the street. They moved as if their limbs all bent the wrong way, awkward and insect-like. I found myself despising them. I hated this place and everything in it. One day I would destroy them all. One day I would make this whole world burn. One day.

But not today.

ThuBOOM.

The ground beneath us gave a faint shudder. The vibrations carried up the bike and along my arms.

ThuBOOM.

'Did you feel that?' Billy asked. Along the street, the creatures had frozen in place, their heads raised. Listening.

ThuBOOM.

A broken slate slid down the roof of the building beside us. It shattered on the ground just a metre or so from the motorbike's front wheel. I watched the broken fragments bounce into the air as the tremors came again.

ThuBOOM.

They were becoming louder now. More slates slipped from the roof. The creatures along the street turned and fled, running away on their ridiculously spindly legs.

ThuBOOM.

ThuBOOM.

ThuBOOM.

'It's speeding up,' I muttered. 'It's like...' My throat tightened as I suddenly realised *exactly* what it was like.

'An earthquake?' Billy suggested.

'No, not an earthquake,' I replied, revving the bike's

engine. 'It's footsteps.'

'*Footsteps?* Footsteps of what?'

Pulling the bike out on to the street, I jabbed a thumb over my shoulder. I felt Billy turn and heard him swear below his breath.

'There's something coming,' he yelped. 'It's... it's...'

'Big and scary and looks like a dinosaur?'

'Yes. How did you know that?'

'We've met.'

The surface of the street was littered with rocks, charred metal and the occasional arm, leg or head that had once belonged to one of the creatures in here. Burning piles of rubbish smoked and spluttered at irregular intervals all the way along it. It wasn't easy to steer the bike through it all, and every second the thunderous footsteps of the creature behind us grew louder.

'We have to ditch the bike,' I announced, cutting off the engine and swinging myself off the leather seat. I yanked off the helmet and let it drop to the ground.

Billy hesitated. I followed his gaze back along the street. The dino-beast was at the village already. Hot tendrils of saliva hung from its jaws and tangled around the four curved tusks. Its pink, beady eyes were fixed on me. I could see the hunger in them, burning and all-consuming.

'*Come on*, Billy,' I hissed, grabbing him by the jumper and hauling him off the bike. 'Don't just sit there. Run!'

Billy got rid of his helmet as I dragged him into the mouth of a narrow alley between two crumbling houses. Shapes whispered, watching us from the darkness. Something sobbed. Boy, girl, it was impossible to tell. A furious roar from the dino-beast silenced them all, and we passed through the alley without any problems.

Before we left the passageway I glanced back out into the street. A foot the size of a steamroller slammed down on to the motorbike. When it lifted, there was nothing but a tangle of metal left on the ground. Mr Preston would be devastated. Assuming he was still alive.

The next street was empty. We sprinted along it – me in front, Billy a few steps behind. The dino-beast's head was visible above the ruined rooftops of the buildings we'd just passed. It swung left to right, its eyes swivelling in their sockets as the monster searched for us.

'How much further is it?' Billy asked. The second he spoke, the dino-beast's head turned sharply. It took a step after us, barely even noticing the two houses. Both buildings crumbled as the creature tore through them. It threw back its ugly head and roared in triumph as it resumed the chase.

'Up the hill,' I wheezed. 'Not far.'

The road had begun to curve steeply upwards. It slowed us down until we were barely going faster than a good walking pace. The dino-beast thudded up behind us, the hill proving no problem for its powerful legs.

I felt the heat of its breath on my back; heard the

chomping of its razor-sharp teeth. Billy and I were side by side now, and I could see my own terror reflected on his face.

With a final effort we reached the top of the hill. My legs burned like fire. My heart machine-gunned in my chest. I sped up, making a sprint for where I knew my house to be.

I heard a grunt behind me, and realised Billy was no longer by my side. I didn't stop, but managed to turn round far enough to see what had happened. Billy was on the ground, face twisted in pain, his hands tight around his ankle.

The dino-beast pounded up the hill, its enormous feet shattering the ground with every step. It'd be on him in seconds. Biting him. Devouring him. Tearing the flesh from his bones.

A whisper swirled inside my head. *Leave him*, it said. *It'll buy you time.*

I saw him lying there. Saw the monster closing on him.

Saw the flecks of blood and foam on its teeth. I stopped running. The voice in my head hissed in disgust. I tried to ignore it, but it was difficult.

If we switched places, would Billy go back for me? Would he risk his own life to save mine? No chance.

Luckily for Billy, I'm not him.

The muscles in my legs tightened like coils as I U-turned and sprinted back towards my fallen classmate. The shadow of the dino-beast flooded the road around us. I didn't dare look up, and instead focused on my feet and on making them go faster.

Saliva poured like fat raindrops on to Billy and me as I threw myself at him. A cloud of hot, choking breath rolled down over us, and I knew the monster's teeth were about to snap shut.

I landed awkwardly next to Billy. My hands clawed out for him. It felt like a lifetime before they found his arm.

The jaws of the beast were closing around us. I glanced

up into the dark passageway of its throat. This was going to be close.

I thought of a spark. Trapped it. Held it. Billy screamed. The monster's teeth clamped shut.

But for the second time that day, it was a second too late.

Chapter Sixteen

HOME SWEET HOME

We opened our eyes and found ourselves in the same spot on the same street in a different reality.

The road beneath us was solid and unbroken. The houses around us were all in good shape. Most importantly, the dino-beast was nowhere to be seen.

'Can you move?' I asked, jumping up.

'After that?' Billy gasped. 'I can hardly speak.' He tried moving his leg, but it was slow going.

'Catch me up,' I said, already running. Billy's knowledge of Caddie might have been useful, but I didn't need him. I could handle her on my own. The sparks were surging through me again. I was primed and ready to fire, and my target was almost in sight.

The door to my house was ajar as I closed in on my front gate. A chill breeze swirled into the hallway, billowing the net curtain into a hazy, ghost-like blob. It was the only movement I could see inside.

My hands caught the posts on either side of the gate and I vaulted over. I didn't notice anything out of the ordinary until I'd landed on the path.

The garden was full of dolls. Dozens of them. Hundreds, maybe. They stood there, still and silent, watching me through painted porcelain eyes. I recognised at once the matching outfits almost all of them wore. It wasn't difficult. After all, I was wearing the same one myself.

My God, I thought. *The faces. I even recognise the faces.*

And I did. There was Darren Woolston from my English class. Over there was Elizabeth... *something*, from the year above. Even Morag the secretary was there, dressed in a miniature version of the same outfit she'd been wearing that morning.

My eyes flitted from face to face, finding dozens I could identify. Every face was different, but the expression on each one was the same. Trapped. Tormented. Haunted.

I tore my eyes from the dolls and hurried for the door. At least I'd found out what had happened to everyone in school, although a big part of me really wished that I hadn't.

'Mum? Mum, are you here?' I yelled, crashing in through the front door and into the little hallway that opened on to the living room.

No answer came.

I hurried through to the kitchen, the tremble in my voice betraying my growing sense of dread. 'Mum? *Mum, where are you?'*

Nothing.

I ran back through to the hallway, where the stairs led to

the upper floor of the house. I was halfway up before I spotted the shape on the living-room floor.

The shape of a person, slumped behind the couch.

I backtracked down the steps, watching the shape through the wooden railings of the stairs. It wasn't moving.

'M-Mum?'

I inched forward, my legs shaking too much for me to move any faster. The couch blocked my view of the shape on the floor, but the image of it was already burned on to my eyes. Dark. Motionless. Mum-sized.

The wheels of the couch gave a *squeak* as I rolled it aside. The shape on the floor still made no move. A black sheet had been thrown on top of it. At first I thought maybe it was just a pile of bedclothes.

Until I saw the hand. It stuck out from beneath the sheet, palm upwards, fingers uncurled. A large patch of blood had dried into the pale brown skin. It wasn't Mum's hand. It wasn't Mum.

It was Ameena.

I dragged the sheet away from her, even though I was terrified of what I might find underneath. I was relieved to discover she was in one piece. Battered and bloody, but more or less intact. A faint groan wheezed through her lips and her eyelids fluttered like butterfly wings.

I didn't speak until her eyes opened all the way.

'What happened?' We both asked the question at the same time. I half expected her to laugh, but she didn't.

'Not sure,' she winced, gingerly propping herself up on to her elbows. 'I remember you asking me to keep an eye on her, and then... Nothing.'

She tried to sit up, but the movement made her eyes lose focus, and she slowly lowered herself back on to the carpet. Just before she did I noticed a bloodstain where her head had been resting.

'Wait there,' I told her. 'I'll get you a drink.'

I stood up, but didn't make it any further. Caddie stood

on the other side of the couch, her dark eyes trained on me. Raggy Maggie was clutched under one arm. In the other hand she held the small kitchen knife Mum uses for chopping vegetables. The knife wasn't big, but it almost looked like a sword in her tiny grip.

'Yay!' she cheered. 'You made it. Your daddy told me you would.'

'Where's my mum?' I demanded.

'I told you,' she said, smirking. 'She's dripping from the ceiling of the—'

Lightning flashed through my brain and the couch flipped into the air. It hit Caddie hard, and slammed her into the wall that divided the living room from the kitchen. She hit the floor with a *thump*.

A few seconds later she crawled out from under the upturned couch, the knife and the doll still in her hands. Only the smile had been dropped.

'I'm going to ask you again,' my voice said, without me

even thinking the words. 'Where's my mum?'

She hesitated long enough to tuck Raggy Maggie back under her arm. Her eyes blazed as she shouted, 'Drip. Drip. Drip.'

Another buzz of electricity passed through me and a tornado swirled around her. It lifted her off her feet and spun her round and round in the middle of the room. Faster and faster it went, until the white and red of her dress blurred into pink.

She lost her grip on the knife and it was spat out by the whirlwind. The blade whistled past me, centimetres from my face. I didn't flinch.

'I'm not playing games,' warned the voice inside me. Was it even my voice at all? 'Tell me where my mum is,' it said. 'Now.'

'Wheee!' Caddie was laughing as she twirled in the air.

My teeth clenched and a high-voltage charge criss-crossed over my skin. The mini-tornado spun faster. It sucked the ornaments from the mantelpiece; ripped pictures from the wall. All the while Caddie's high giggle filled the room.

'WHERE IS SHE?'

The wind dropped, but Caddie didn't. Sparks of blue flashed behind my eyes and she slammed against the wall. I felt rage uncoiling like a snake in my gut. It told me to hurt her. Told me to shut her up, stop her laughing.

My eye gave a twitch and her arms bent back until they were by her head. She was pinned against the plaster like an insect. Her mouth was still fixed in a grin, but her eyes told another story.

Another buzz at the base of my skull and I saw the muscles in her throat go tight. The smile vanished almost at once as she hung there, fighting against her slowly collapsing windpipe.

'This was always just a game to you, wasn't it?' I said. 'What was that rule you made again? Not to use my

abilities, wasn't it?' I felt my lips draw back into a smile.
'Oops.'

'O-OK,' she managed to wheeze. 'I'll tell you.'

I ignored her. The power bounced around excitedly inside me. It was loving every minute of this.

And so was I.

'I'll t-tell you where she is.'

Her face had lost its chalky whiteness and was turning purple before my eyes. I squeezed tighter. Could I make her head pop, I wondered? It would be fun to find out.

'She's... up... upstairs.'

I felt my lips move; heard my voice speak. 'Who is?'

Caddie's head tilted quizzically to one side. She looked at me with something close to fear in her eyes. The look jolted me, and I suddenly remembered my reason for being there.

'M-Mum,' I whispered. The word staggered out of the fog at the back of my mind. At once the blue flashes stopped. Caddie gave a yelp as she dropped to the floor.

I'd forgotten her. I'd been so fixed on hurting Caddie I'd forgotten about Mum. My dad was right – I *was* just like him. I did have a darkness inside me, and I had almost let it consume me completely.

'Kyle, look out!' Ameena cried. She was on her knees, using the windowsill to pull herself up. Her eyes were on the door at my back.

I spun round, fists raised, no idea what I'd be faced with. A hunched figure just a little taller than myself limped in through the doorway.

'Billy,' I said, sighing with relief. I took a step closer to help support him. 'Come on, I think they're upstai—'

It started as a pin-prick, just to the left of my belly button. I barely felt the rest of the kitchen knife's blade slide into my stomach – until the top of the wooden handle pressed against me.

'Surprise,' Billy grinned, and I saw the devil was back in his eyes.

I felt a tug at my trousers. In shock I turned. Caddie looked up at me, her dark eyes nothing more than narrow slits in her face.

'Billy's *my* friend,' she snarled. 'Not yours.'

As if to prove this, Billy gave his hand a sharp twist to the right. The blade in my belly turned, opening my wound up wide. Pain exploded through my body, rampaging up and bursting from my mouth as a scream.

'B-but... what she did...' I babbled. 'What she did to you.'

'I deserved it,' Billy replied. 'All of it. I was a bad boy for forgetting her. A very bad boy. Bad boys must be punished.'

There was no use trying to reason with him. Either Billy was brainwashed or he was mad. Whichever, it wasn't good news for me.

I caught him by the shoulders and pushed, trying to get him away. He staggered backwards on his twisted ankle, but managed to catch hold of me. Together we stumbled out through the front door and into the garden.

He missed the step and landed badly on his injured foot. As we fell he threw out his hands to protect himself, letting go of the knife. Somehow I managed to twist my body so I crunched down on to my shoulder, avoiding landing on the handle that stuck out of me.

Static hissed in my ears like a badly tuned radio. I could feel my heart beating in my stomach, pumping blood from my wound. All around me the painted faces of my classmates watched on, unblinking.

Billy was under a metre away, lying half on the path and half on the grass, gripping his leg just above the ankle. I could hear him swearing. I'd heard his bone give a *crack* when he'd fallen off the step. I hoped it was broken. And I hoped it hurt. Badly.

My fingers crawled down my body like spiders. I gave a whimper as my hands found the handle of the kitchen knife. The pain was immense. It burned like lava through my insides.

The edges of the world were becoming soft and indistinct. I rolled on to my back. Wispy grey dragons circled far overhead. I watched them for a while, until they merged with other clouds and took on different shapes.

Their movements were soothing. Relaxing. They swam in the sky like lullabies, miles away yet close enough to touch. I watched them dancing to the hissing in my head, and felt the fire in my belly die down. The clouds left a faint, silvery trail behind them as they twirled and weaved across the heavens.

My eyes followed them. Their patterns were beautiful. I felt as if I could watch them for ever. Like I had all the time in the world.

But I knew I didn't.

My fingers tightened around the knife's wooden handle. I said goodbye to the dragons. And then I pulled.

The hole was wide and the knife slid out easily. Easily, but far from painlessly. It dragged my top half up with it. I screamed, bursting the bubbles of spit that had formed on my lips.

The knife hit the path with a dull clatter. A spurt of blood spat from my belly, turning my red jumper a darker shade of crimson. Somewhere inside the house Ameena screamed. Far overhead an icy wind swept all the lullabies away.

I closed my eyes and tried to imagine a bandage across the stab wound. Every time I got close to visualising it, though, another wave of pain crashed down on me, washing the image away. The sparks buzzed inside me, but they were all moving in different directions, confused and disorientated.

I held a hand over the hole, pressing it as tightly as I could bear. With my other arm I tried to manoeuvre myself into a position from where I could stand up.

Billy's head turned sharply as he saw what I was doing. He tried to twist, arms outstretched, reaching for me. I managed to fire out a kick. It caught him under the chin and snapped his head further back. He gave a short cry, followed by a soft groan. There was no need to kick him again. He was out cold.

I shuffled on to my knees, head hanging down, one hand resting on the path for support. I wasted ten seconds getting my breath back, then lifted my head and got ready to move.

One of the dolls was right by my face. Its glassy gaze stared past me, to where the gate flapped in the breeze. As I watched, the doll slowly turned its head in my direction. Its expressionless porcelain face pulled into an impossibly wide grin.

'Peek-a-boo,' it chimed. 'I see you.'

Chapter Seventeen

DOLL'S HOUSE

I was bent at the waist as I half ran, half tripped back into the house. My left hand was still clutching the wound in my belly. With the right I caught the edge of the door and closed it with a *slam*.

And not a second too soon. Every doll in the garden had started to move as I'd pulled myself to my feet. I could already hear them sniggering and giggling as they hurled themselves against the door. I could already see them on the window ledge, their faces stretched into wicked smiles. They were battering their heads against the glass; kicking at the panes with their tiny plastic shoes. It would've seemed funny if it wasn't so damned terrifying.

'Kyle!' Ameena flew at me and caught me under the arm. I leaned into her, relieved no longer to have to stand on my own. She pulled gently at my hand, then quickly pressed it back against me as the blood began to seep out. 'Jesus,' she fretted, and I noticed for the first time that her face was criss-crossed with deep scratches. 'You need a hospital.'

'So... so do you.'

'It's nothing,' she shrugged. 'But you... you're in bad shape.'

The door began to shake in its frame and we lumbered further away from it. The letterbox opened with a faint creak, and a spindly stuffed arm reached in. It grasped at the air for a few seconds, before slowly retracting.

'You know,' Ameena muttered, 'that was *almost* cute.'

'Your face,' I wheezed. 'Caddie?'

'She tried to follow you out to the garden, but I caught

her,' Ameena explained. 'Little witch went crazy. Lashed out.' She traced the contours of one of the deeper slashes. 'Her fingernails are sharper than they look.'

'Where is she?' I asked, looking towards the stairs. 'Did she get away?'

'Come on,' smiled Ameena. She nodded over to the corner of the room, where a Caddie-sized bundle lay slumped on the floor. 'Psychotic demon-child or not, one good knee to the head and she drops like anyone else.'

'Way to go,' I congratulated. 'You beat up a five-year-old.'

Ameena chewed her lip. 'Wow. Actually it does sound pretty bad when you put it like that...'

The room was growing darker as more and more dolls piled up by the windows. They were clambering over one another, trying to reach the glass. Trying to break through.

'You know there're a thousand evil-looking dolls

hammering on your windows, right?'

'I'd noticed,' I breathed. 'Think it's only about six hundred.'

'Oh.' Ameena considered this. 'That's not so bad then.' She followed my gaze as I glanced across to the telephone. For once it had been put back on the charger. 'Line's dead,' she told me. 'I already checked.'

I turned in the direction of the stairs. The movement hurt. A lot.

'Let me take a look at that,' Ameena frowned, her eyes falling to where blood was seeping through my fingers.

'It's fine,' I lied. 'It wasn't a big knife. It was just—'

Pit-pat-pit-pat. Something small and fast-moving zipped across the living-room floor. I barely spotted it in the corner of my eye before it vanished beneath the coffee table.

'Did you see that?' I whispered.

Ameena nodded. 'I saw something.'

We watched the table for a few long moments. Nothing

moved. Whatever had gone under there was staying where it was.

'Go upstairs,' I whispered. 'Make sure my mum and Lilly are there.'

'What? Are you crazy? You don't know what's under there, and look at you, you're—'

'Ameena, please,' I implored, turning to her. 'I need to know my mum's OK. I need you to keep her safe. Her and Lilly. You're the only one I can trust to do it.' I forced my face into something close to a smile. 'You're the trusty sidekick, remember?'

She thought about arguing. I knew she wanted to, but something on my face must've told her she couldn't possibly win.

'Be careful,' she told me, as she made for the stairs. 'I'll shout if she's there.'

I turned back to the coffee table. Outside, the dolls of my schoolmates giggled like hyenas as they continued to hurl themselves against the windows and door.

Blood dripped through my fingers and on to the carpet as I inched forward. The pain locked my teeth together and tightened my free hand into a fist. I needed medical help, and I needed it fast. But right now there was no possible way of getting it.

The electric blue sparks were still buzzing around inside me, but they were still erratic and confused, like bats lost in the daytime. I couldn't harness them, but then I wasn't even sure if I wanted to.

The sense of power had been overwhelming. I'd felt drunk on it, like nothing in the world mattered but me and my abilities. My mum was in danger, and I'd forgotten.

No, worse – I hadn't even cared.

'They're here.' Ameena's voice was muffled by the ceiling above me, but I heard her loud and clear. 'They're tied up, but they're OK.'

'Untie them and stay with them,' I said, as loudly as I

could manage. 'Keep them safe.'

'Ten-four.'

At least Mum was in good hands now. Even if anything happened to me, I knew I could count on Ameena to protect her.

I shuffled forward until I was less than a metre from the table. I lowered myself to my knees, being as careful as I could not to jolt my body and make my wound even worse. Cautious as I was, the pain flared like fire, and I had to catch hold of the tabletop to avoid falling on to my face.

The room was almost silent as I bent forward. Even the relentless hammering of the dolls outside seemed to ease off, as if they had stopped trying to get in and were all now just watching me.

As the floor beneath the table came into view I saw... nothing. Nothing but empty carpet. I bent further, pushing through the pain, until I could see the underside of the tabletop itself. There was nothing hiding there, either.

Whatever had been under the table had come back out.

So where was it now?

Down there on my knees I suddenly felt very vulnerable. Using the table, I pushed myself back up into a standing position, ignoring the dizziness and nausea the sudden movement brought on.

Pit-pat-pit-pat. It came again, somewhere off to my left. I turned, but saw nothing. *Pit-pat-pit-pat.* Where had it come from this time? Somewhere close by, but...

Pit-pat-pit-pat. The scampering was very close now. Outside the dolls had begun hammering on the windows with even more force. They sniggered and chattered, their porcelain heads wobbling excitedly on their soft shoulders.

Another laugh – high and scratchy, like a witch's cackle – made itself heard above the rattling of the windowpane. This laugh was louder. This laugh was here, inside the room.

Directly above me.

I craned my neck and looked up. I barely had time to recognise the single eye of Raggy Maggie before she landed on my face.

The doll cackled as she lashed out at me. I caught her with my free hand and tried to yank her off, but her dirty, tattered legs were latched on to my throat. She lurched at my eye, her mouth open. I saw a flash of pin-like teeth, and barely managed to pull back before they snapped shut.

My fingers wrapped around one of Raggy Maggie's legs. It felt solid and strong as I heaved against it. The doll screeched and wriggled, but I managed to tear the leg from my neck.

With a flick of my wrist I sent her spinning across the room. She bounced off the wall with a *crack*. When she hit the carpet she only had part of her head left.

It didn't stop her.

The half-face she had left twisted into a furious scowl. She kept her one-eyed stare on me as she scurried along the floor, staying close to the wall.

I watched her, swaying slightly, the high-speed pumping of my heart spilling more blood out of my stomach.

'You're a bad boy,' Raggy Maggie grimaced. I could see Caddie from where I was standing. Even though the girl still appeared unconscious, her lips moved in time with her doll's. 'You're a very bad boy, and you know what happens to bad boys, don't you?'

I realised too late where she was heading. I stumbled forward, but even without the hole in my belly I wouldn't have been fast enough to stop her.

'Bad boys get *punished*,' she screeched. And with that, she leapt up, caught the door handle, and pulled it open. A tumbling sea of red pushed in, tiny arms outstretched, faces stretched into a cruel mockery of a grin.

Backing away, I found the coffee table. I clumsily clambered on to it, as dozens of demented dolls flooded my living room. They pushed past and fell over each other as they rushed to get at me, their beady eyes glazed with wicked delight.

The top of the table was taller than the dolls were, but it didn't take long for one to climb up. I recognised it as Mark Simpson, one of Billy's cohorts. The satisfaction I felt when I toe-punted him across the room almost made the whole experience seem worthwhile.

Another doll made it up, then another. I kicked them both away, but others rushed to take their place. No matter how hard I booted them, they immediately rejoined the throng, falling over themselves to reach me.

Four dolls made it on to the table at the same time. I lashed out, sweeping my leg around in an arc, and managed to send them all flying. The move took its toll on me, though, and I had to fight to keep my footing on the table.

I couldn't keep this up for long. Any second now they were going to knock me off. I could almost feel them swarming over me, their tiny hands and feet gouging me, tearing at me.

I wanted to shout for help, but what if the dolls didn't know about Mum upstairs? What if my shouts gave her away? I couldn't risk it, so I kept my mouth shut.

Tiny arms wrapped round my leg before I knew what was happening. I turned, but the doll clung on and moved with me. I looked down into the painted face of Mr Jones, my geography teacher. I saw his mouth snap open, heard him hiss, and felt his jagged teeth sink into my calf.

Even as I stumbled, the table was wobbling. Some of the dolls were under it, pushing up, lifting it off the floor. My arm flailed wildly as I fought to stay balanced, but it was no use. The floor became the ceiling as I flipped over and landed in the middle of a frenzy of snapping jaws.

I kicked out, but for every doll I hit I missed fifty more. They were all over me, tiny hands and feet digging into every part of my body. Teeth chomping through my clothes, searching for my flesh.

They pinned my arms, exposing the wound in my stomach. They caught hold of my thrashing legs. I kicked out with even more fury, sending half a dozen of them hurtling away, but twenty, sixty, *a hundred* more hands caught my ankles and forced them to the floor.

They caught my ears and they pulled my hair, stopping me moving my head. Only my eyes were mine to control, but I shut them, too terrified to look at the disturbingly familiar faces of the dolls.

A clutch of tiny hands tilted my head backwards, as I had done to Ameena's when I thought she was dead. I doubted I was in for the kiss of life, though. The dolls, I was sure, had something far nastier in mind.

I heard a giggle by my shoulder, felt a sharp pressure against my throat and braced myself for the end.

'Stop it.' The voice floated over from somewhere near

the couch. The sting of the teeth against my throat eased off at once, but the other dolls continued to hold me down.

I opened my eyes. Caddie was standing above me. Raggy Maggie was perched on her shoulder. Both of them looked down, their faces wearing matching expressions of contempt.

'Let him go.' The girl and her doll both said the words at the same time. Two mouths. One voice.

At once I felt the pressure of a thousand tiny hands leave me. I moved to get up, but an icicle stabbed through my brain again and my whole body went limp. Without any effort, Caddie had pinned me down far more effectively than the dolls could ever have done.

'There are people up the stairs,' Caddie and Raggy Maggie told the chattering dolls. 'Get them. Bring them down.' Her narrow eyebrows crawled halfway up her forehead. 'He's going to watch them die.'

Chapter Eighteen

SUDDEN DEATH

The dolls of my classmates sniggered as they swarmed off up the stairs. I lay there, powerless to stop them. Powerless to protect my mum.

In just a few seconds, all the dolls that had come into the house had disappeared upstairs, leaving me alone with Caddie, Raggy Maggie... and the knife in Caddie's hand.

The dolls' heads had blocked the kitchen knife from my view, but now I could see it all too clearly. The blade was red with my blood. It dripped along the metal and sploshed on to the carpet beside my head. The wound in my gut throbbed sharply, as if remembering how the knife had felt.

'Your daddy said you'd play rough.' Caddie knelt next to me on the carpet. Raggy Maggie swung down from her shoulder and landed on my chest. Now it was half broken, I could see right inside the doll's porcelain head. It was completely smooth and empty, with no brain or anything else to speak of.

But that didn't make her any less alive. As Caddie continued speaking to me, the doll crawled down my chest to my stomach.

'But I don't think you're so tough,' Caddie said. She leaned in closer to me, so her face was almost touching mine. 'I think you're just a big baby,' she whispered.

Agony went off like a bomb in my stomach, as Raggy Maggie wriggled an arm or a leg – I couldn't tell which – into my stab wound. The coldness inside my head had my whole body frozen, so I couldn't even open my mouth, couldn't even scream.

Caddie put one hand on my forehead, steadying

herself. She raised the knife, holding the point a few centimetres above my heart. She and Raggy Maggie giggled at the same time, but behind it I noticed another sound too. The fast thudding of hundreds of tiny footsteps running down the stairs.

I heard a woman's voice cry out: 'Get away from her. Leave us alone!'

Mum. The electrical power inside me buzzed furiously, but it was still disjointed and erratic. Too random and chaotic to harness.

Caddie's head rotated like an owl's, until it was completely facing the other way. We both watched as the dolls flooded down the stairs, their rigid hands carrying Mum, Ameena and a little girl I guessed was Lilly above their heads.

'Oh, look,' Caddie sang. 'It's Mummy. You're just in time.'

'Kyle!' Mum yelped. She thrashed against the dolls, but

every time she came close to getting up they dragged her back down.

Ameena too was lashing out. She was grabbing at the tiny figures, hurling any she caught across the room. Each one thudded against the wall, dropped to the floor, then scurried back over to rejoin the pack.

Only Lilly wasn't fighting. She was holding herself still. Her mouth was open and her eyes were screwed shut. She was crying so hard no sound was coming out.

'Put them down,' Caddie commanded. The dolls immediately set their prisoners down on the floor. 'Now go away. These are *ours* to play with.'

Like a shoal of fish, the dolls all turned in unison and made for the door. Mum jumped up even before Ameena did. I'd never in my life seen her looking as angry as she did when she threw herself towards Caddie.

Halfway there, a strange, shocked look flashed across my mum's face. Her legs buckled under her and she dropped to the floor. She lay there, motionless, except for her eyes, which flicked helplessly around the room before settling on me. I could see the pain in them. The sorrow. The fear. And it nearly killed me.

'Lilly, stay down,' Ameena roared. She leapt over my Mum, drawing back a fist as she closed in on Caddie.

For a moment I thought she was going to make it. But then the same expression of shock was on her face, and she was slumping on to the floor just a metre or two away from me.

Caddie's head swivelled back until she was looking at me again. Her hand pressed down harder on my head. Raggy Maggie scuttled up Caddie's arm and perched on her shoulder. What remained of the doll's face was lit up with a barbaric glee.

'You know what's the tricky part?' Caddie asked. 'Picking who I'm going to kill first.'

She kept her eyes on me while she stood up. She raised

the knife until it was pointing towards Ameena. I watched helplessly as she began to move the knife from Ameena to Lilly to Mum, then back to Ameena again.

'My mummy and your mummy were hanging out the clothes,' she sang, the knife switching target with every word. 'My mummy gave your mummy a punch on the nose. What colour was the blood to be?'

The knife stopped. Caddie's head twisted round to see who had been chosen to die first.

'Oh, look,' she said. 'It's your mummy!'

I met Mum's gaze with my own. Her eyes were shiny with tears. She didn't look away from me, not even when Caddie's shadow fell across her face.

'After this it's your girlfriend,' Caddie told me through a giggle.

The power rushed through my body in every direction at once. The pain and the fear had shattered my control. There was no way I could make it do anything I wanted.

'W-wait.' The word came slurred from my mouth. Caddie's eyes widened a little, as if surprised I'd managed to speak at all. 'My dad,' I murmured, 'he... he's using you.'

Caddie seemed to think about this for a second, then her shoulders raised in a shrug. 'Oh well,' she said, turning her attention back to my mum.

'The Darkest Corners,' I gasped. Caddie froze at the name. 'He'll... he'll b-bring you back.'

'No, he won't!' Caddie turned on me like a wild animal, her face contorted into a snarl. 'I'm never going back to that place,' she snapped. 'Never *ever*.'

'He w-will,' I insisted. Just making my voice box work was agonisingly difficult, but I forced the words to come. 'When he's done w-with you he'll take you back.'

'Shut up,' the girl hissed, the knife trembling in her hand as she pointed it at me. 'Shut up right now.'

'You'll be stuck there,' I told her. 'Trapped. F-for ever.'

'*I said shut up!*' She flew at me, knife drawn back by her ear. Raggy Maggie clung on to her neck, her broken face fixed in a mask of hatred.

Caddie's hand slapped down on my head. Her teeth were clenched tight, and flecks of spittle bubbled at the corners of her mouth. Her narrowed eyes fixed on the centre of my chest. I had a second – maybe two – before she plunged the knife into my heart. I couldn't control the sparks colliding in my head. I couldn't make my power work.

But I didn't have to. All I had to do was concentrate. All I had to do was ignore the burning in my belly and the terror in my throat and trap one spark.

The knife and Caddie's hand began to move.

I thought of Mum.

The rest was easy.

The carpet at my back went first, followed by the patterned paper on the walls. I watched the ceiling disappear. The bedroom above vanished too, followed by the attic. In the blink of an eye I was looking up at a sky full of black, swirling clouds.

In just a few seconds the whole room had changed into a dark mirror-image of itself. No, not just the whole room.

The whole world.

Caddie's snarl caught in her throat and her hand stopped, mid-way to my chest. Terror lit up her eyes, and I felt the cold fog lift from inside my head. My muscles relaxed. I could move again.

'We're... we're...' she stammered.

'You're home,' I told her.

'No,' she sobbed. 'It's not fair. Take us back. Take us back!'

The hand holding the knife trembled, its knuckles bony white. She caught me by the hair and held the blade just a few centimetres from my eye.

'Take us back,' she hissed. 'You'd better take us back *right now.*'

I didn't answer. Instead, I put two fingers in my mouth and blew. A shrill whistle rose into the night.

ThuBOOM.

Caddie froze. Raggy Maggie's grip tightened on the girl's shoulder. 'What was that?' they whispered together.

ThuBOOM.

I shifted my weight and caught hold of the hand holding the knife.

ThuBOOM.

'To be honest,' I said, 'I'm not sure what it's called.'

An enormous shape appeared above the broken walls of my house, blocking out the sky. Clouds of hot air billowed from the dino-beast's flared nostrils.

'But it sure looks hungry.'

With a grunt I pushed Caddie away. She and the doll both screamed as they were thrown backwards on to the dirty wooden floorboards.

The monster lunged, its jaws open – wide enough to

swallow all three of us. My focus slammed shut around another spark in my head.

In a heartbeat I flitted between the two worlds, and as I did Caddie's scream echoed across them both.

The carpet felt soft against my back. I lay there, unmoving, eyes fixed on the ceiling above me. I could hear Ameena moving. Behind her, Mum was already getting to her feet.

'Kyle!' she cried. 'What happened? Where did you go?'

She was by my side, arms over me, hugging me tight. It hurt like hell, but I didn't ever want it to stop.

'Long story,' I wheezed. 'Maybe... I can tell you about it later.'

She pulled away and looked at me. Her tears fell down on me like raindrops. 'Everything,' she nodded. 'We'll talk about everything.'

Her head came down as she hugged me again, and I

saw Ameena standing behind her. A little girl with wispy blonde hair was in her arms. Lilly's head was tucked in tight against Ameena's neck, and her crystal blue eyes were wide with fear.

'You did it then,' Ameena said with a nod.

'I did it.'

She gave my leg a friendly poke with her toe. 'Nice going.' Ameena glanced at the window, then back down at me. A smile tugged at the corners of her mouth. 'You know you've got about a thousand really confused school kids outside your house, right?'

I lifted my head and looked across to the window. I could make out a mass of red jumpers milling around in the garden. 'Only about six hundred.'

'Oh,' she said. 'Well, then that's not so bad...'

It took a lot to convince Mum not to take me to the hospital. In the end she agreed that they'd ask too many questions about how I'd come to have a four-centimetre stab wound in my stomach.

We decided she would clean it and dress it as best she could. If it got worse, she said, then she'd drag me to the hospital kicking and screaming if she had to. I agreed. It was the best deal I was going to get.

When we came to examine the wound, though, it didn't look too bad. It felt a little better too, and it wasn't long before I realised why.

Mesmerised, we watched the skin gradually knitting itself back together. It wasn't happening fast, but it was definitely happening. The hole was closing over. The injury was mending itself right before our eyes.

'How are you doing that?' Mum asked in a hushed whisper.

'I'm not,' I said. 'I mean, I don't think I am. Not on purpose, anyway.'

We were in the kitchen now – me standing by the table,

Mum kneeling in front of me, studying the hole in my belly.

'Incredible,' Mum whispered. She gazed at the closing wound for a few more seconds, then gave her head a shake. 'I'm going to put a dressing on it anyway,' she said.

'OK.'

She began wiping round the wound with a foul-smelling green liquid. It hurt almost as much as the knife had.

'So,' Mum said, dabbing at the dried blood, 'your friend...'

'What about her?'

'She seems... nice.'

'She's not my girlfriend, if that's what you're going to ask,' I said.

'Perish the thought,' Mum smiled. She finished wiping the blood away and began applying some gauze and cotton wool. 'Where does she live? Your friend. What's her name again?'

'Ameena.'

'That's it. Where does she live?'

I shrugged, earning myself a 'Keep still.'

'Nowhere, really,' I said. 'She's pretty much homeless.'

Mum nodded. The tape for the dressing felt sticky and tight as she pressed it to my skin.

'You know,' she said, not looking up at me, 'Nan's room isn't doing anything at the minute.'

I glanced through to the living room. Ameena had moved the couch back into position and was now sitting on it, Lilly still nestled in her arms. I couldn't have held my smile back if I'd tried.

'Thanks, Mum,' I whispered. 'You're the best.'

I stood in the doorway of Nan's old room, not quite sure what to say. Ameena was standing by the bed, looking at it as if it might explode at any minute. The light from the full moon outside illuminated the hideous flower pattern of the bedsheets.

'Mum says she'll get you other covers,' I said, seeing Ameena's expression. 'They're a bit... old-fashioned.'

'What? No, they're fine, they're great, it's just...'

'Just what?' I asked, my hands wringing nervously together. 'Is it the curtains? We can probably change them too if you don't—'

'Calm down, it's not the curtains, either.'

'Well... what then?'

'It's just been a long time since I slept in a bed,' she said. 'A proper actual bed.'

She lowered herself down on to it and sighed. But it was a sigh of happiness and contentment.

'Goodnight then,' I said, watching her lie back and slowly close her eyes.

'Night, kiddo,' she said.

'Sleep tight.'

She opened one eye. 'I will if you shut up for five minutes.'

We both smiled, and I closed the door, leaving her to her dreams.

Her room was directly across the landing from mine. Mum had gone to bed over an hour ago – just before midnight – so I tiptoed to my own room and quietly closed the door.

I slid the curtains closed, blocking out the view of the Keller House, where I'd faced off against Mr Mumbles just two weeks ago. My encounter with him had seemed like a nightmare at the time, but I'd take him over Caddie, Raggy Maggie and an army of evil dolls any day.

As I pulled back my covers I found myself wondering what the kids and teachers from my school must be thinking right now. From what I could gather none of them had the foggiest idea how they'd arrived in my garden. As far as they were concerned they were in school one moment, and milling around outside my house the next. Their collective amnesia would no doubt make the papers, but hopefully the finger of suspicion wouldn't end up pointing back at me.

Mrs Milton was fine too, if the mystery man was to be believed. I wasn't sure what to make of him yet, and I hoped I'd get a chance to ask him some questions. I didn't think he was lying to me, though, and even though she was a bit of a battleaxe, it was good to know the headmistress was safe.

So that left only Billy. When we'd taken Lilly home I'd asked her mum if Billy was in. She said he wasn't, but as we walked away I spotted his bedroom curtains twitch. For just a moment I saw him there through the gap, glaring down at me. The curtains shifted again, and Billy vanished behind them once more.

I knew he was in bad shape physically, and probably worse shape mentally. He needed help. Despite everything that had happened between us, I hoped he'd be OK.

My sheets felt cold as I slipped under my duvet. I tucked

my knees up near my chest and snuggled in. There was no pain in my stomach now. I'd peeked beneath the dressing an hour or so after Mum had put it on, and the wound just wasn't there any more. The power inside me felt back under control now. I could feel it buzzing inside me, eager to be put to use.

Too eager. My abilities may have repaired my injuries, but they were dangerous. For a short while today they had turned me into someone else. Someone I didn't like. I decided there and then I would never use them again.

'I'm going to offer you one last chance.' The voice came from over near my door. I sat up in bed and saw my dad standing in the corner of the room. 'Join me and all this can stop.' He walked over and sat on the end of the bed. I watched him, too shocked to speak.

'You nearly died today,' he continued. 'Your mother nearly died.'

'And whose fault was that?' I spat.

'I never wanted you or your mother hurt,' he said. 'I just wanted you to live up to your potential. Caddie strayed from the plan. Don't blame me.'

'None of this would have happened if you hadn't sent her.'

My dad sighed. 'It doesn't have to be like this, Kyle,' he said, his voice soft and soothing. 'We can all be together. Working together. Side by side.'

'Working together to take over the world,' I pointed out.

'Not *taking over* the world,' he said. 'Reshaping it. Making it new. Making it *better*.' He reached over and stroked my hair. His hand felt warm. It felt good. I hated him for it. 'We'd be a family,' he smiled. 'Isn't that what you always wanted? You'd have a mum *and* a dad.'

'I've got a family,' I said, not even bothering to disguise the croak in my voice. I shuffled back in my bed and his hand fell away from me. 'It's single-parent.'

His face darkened and for a moment I thought he was

going to make a lunge for me. Instead he just nodded.

'Very well,' he said, standing up. 'That was my last offer. Everything that happens next – every terrible thing that happens to you and your mum and everyone you have ever cared about – is your fault, boy. *Yours.*' He pulled himself up to his full, impressive height. 'What do you say to *that*?'

I felt my skin tingle with electricity. The power soared and swam through my insides, flowing smoothly, like the workings of a perfectly balanced machine. My abilities were growing. They wouldn't take over next time, I would make sure. I could control them. I could make them do *anything.*

'Good luck,' I told him. And then I yawned, turned over, and happily surrendered to the welcoming arms of sleep.